Murder Among The Rich

A Nash Adams Mystery

Written by G.L. Gracie

Murder Among the Rich
By G.L. Gracie
© 2016 Published by G.L. Gracie
Formatting and Graphics by Leah Banicki

https://www.facebook.com/G.L.Gracie

Chapter 1

Sounds of the electric fan struggling to make some kind of headway against the early spring heat wave pierced the air in the stuffy little room Nash Adams called his office. He watched as blossoms from the flowering tree outside the open window drifted to the ground. A small radio belting out the latest popular music and the drone of the fan were the only sounds in the sparsely decorated room. But there was a lot of activity going on in Nash's head.

He had started out with ambitions of becoming a lawyer. However, part way through his second year of college, his father's unexpected death left Nash with the responsibility for the care of his mother and younger sister and little brother. Pop hadn't really considered what would happen if he died and hadn't thought ahead to provide for his family. Midge, Nash's sister, had been hired at a local dress shop; and, although she didn't make much money, every little bit helped. Midge's dreams of going to college and becoming a nurse had been put on hold as well. Ted was a junior attending Cannon High School and Nash intended that he stay there until he graduated. Jobs were hard enough to come by these days and Ted needed that high school diploma.

So Nash Adams had decided to open his own business as was clearly stated on the glass door of the tiny room. Nash Adams, Personal Investigator.

He had chosen to use the word personal rather than private, thinking that might be more appealing to potential clients and perhaps catch their attention.

Well, here he was, ready and willing, but it wasn't that easy to find those clients. He had advertisements posted in all the places he could think of...the local groceries, the library, the gas station, the 7-11 convenience store on the corner, Mr. Meijer's deli. His buddy, Louie, on the police force had even taken one of the posters down to the precinct. Paying for big time advertising was out of the question right now.

Information from the half dozen cases or so he had managed to obtain was stored in file folders in the dented metal file cabinet he'd picked up at a second hand store across town, the same place where he'd purchased the wooden desk which held his feet at this particular moment. With hands placed behind his head and leaning back in his desk chair, he inhaled the fragrant aroma of the narcissus growing outside the window. Those and the flowering tree were the only signs of green in the entire area. Concrete and litter had taken over most of the neighborhood. But this was a space he could afford and he wasn't about to go out and spend money he didn't have.

A black phone rested silently on the wooden desk, his newly acquired camera was in the second drawer of the file cabinet and his gun was in the top drawer of the desk. A flip calendar, one that was free from the lumber company down the street, was open on the top of his desk to cover up the initials someone had carved into the top surface; and a clipboard and pencil were at the ready. Now all he needed was some customers. And hopefully that would happen before the rent came due.

Maybe no one would want to climb the wooden stairs to his second floor office. But rent for the second floor was cheaper and would have to do for the time being. Sharing space on the second floor was a talent agency. At least that's what it said on the door. He hadn't met the man who occupied that office yet. And, of course, the Meijer delicatessen was on the first floor and Mr. Meijer was the landlord who had been sympathetic enough to Nash's situation to reduce the rent by five dollars per month to help out the struggling new businessman. Nash appreciated his kindness. Even at five dollars less per month, the rent would still be tight. The Meijer family...Mr. Meijer, Mrs. Meijer and their teen-age daughter, Anne...lived on the floor level in the three tiny rooms behind the deli.

Nash brushed back the shock of light brown hair which continued to fall over his perspiring forehead. His body was lean like that of a runner. Well, he still did run almost every morning; but that, too, sometimes had to be put on hold, taking second place to more pressing matters. A sigh escaped his mouth as he closed his light blue eyes in an attempt to block out the issues that surrounded his day-to-day existence.

At first he wasn't sure he'd heard a knock on the door; but before he could comprehend, the door opened and through it came the most beautiful woman he'd ever seen. His feet hit the floor with a sudden thud as the chair came to an upright position.

She floated through the doorway and across the room to his desk. In one instant, he took in the marvelous body wrapped in the red skirt topped with the lacey blouse. From there his eyes traveled to the red lips and the raven colored hair which caressed her face and then cascaded to slightly brush her shoulders. Her eyes were the bluest he'd ever seen and her lips were red with lipstick. Oh, yeah, he'd noticed that before. Gold hoop earrings dangled near her cheeks and when she smiled, the red lipstick was very inviting.

He managed to get to his feet; but before he could say anything, she extended a hand decorated with an assortment of rings, some of which he was sure were very expensive. A gold bracelet slid down to her delicate wrist. Taking her extended hand, he looked into the sparkling blue eyes and the sparsely decorated room seemed to disappear from view.

"Mr. Adams?" she smiled.

His mouth was extremely dry.

"Yes," he stuttered. "Yes. Nash Adams."

Carefully withdrawing her hand, she smiled at him once again. Such a beguiling smile.

"My name is Gina..."

Nash was concentrating on the name. Gina had to be the most beautiful name he'd ever heard.

"...Gina Woods. And my husband is missing."

With that, Gina Woods pulled out a silky handkerchief and proceeded to dab at her eyes.

Oh, husband. Wow!

Nash recovered enough to form the words.

"How can I help?"

Did that sound professional? Probably not.

He wanted to offer her a chair, but realized the only chair in the room was the desk chair. Perhaps he needed to think about getting a second chair.

She was talking again.

"I fear something has happened to him and the police have not been able to help me and I thought perhaps someone of your experience and expertise…"

Questioning both of those qualities, but feeling his ego growing, he finally smiled back at the red lips.

"You've come to the right place."

How could he be so out of breath? It wasn't like he'd been running a race or anything.

"I knew that the moment I walked in," she paused with a sigh, apparently putting aside the appearance of the meager room. "Do you think you could fit my dilemma into your schedule?"

Could he fit her into his schedule? Oh, my! Certainly! He floundered with his calendar, pretending to check his appointments.

"Looks like you're in luck. I seem to be available," he said as a red blush crept up his neck.

"I'll need some information," he said as he fumbled for his pencil and tablet.

Gina made herself comfortable by placing one hip of her red skirt on the edge of his desk. Nash swallowed as he became conscious of the curve of her leg.

Gina's husband, Stephen, had been missing for 48 hours. She couldn't think of any reason for his absence. He hadn't been in contact with or been seen by any of their close friends or family. By the time they had finished their conversation, Nash had a list of names of family and friends and a list of places Mr. Woods could be, among them a hunting lodge in the mountains, a beach house in Alabama, a cottage in the east and of course the house on Hickory Lane.

Best of all, Gina Woods opened her check book; and without asking about his fee, plunked down a sizeable check which looked out of place on the scratched wooden desk.

"This ought to be enough to get you started. Let me know when you need more."

With that, Gina Woods slithered off the desk and made her way towards the door while Nash watched how the red skirt pulled across her hips as she walked in the three-inch platform heels. She paused as she opened the door and turned towards him.

"Thank you, Mr. Adams…Nash…" she purred. "I knew the minute I saw you that you are the man for the job."

And Gina Woods was out the door. The last thing Nash remembered about her visit was the red lipstick.

———————◆◆◆———————

Music from the radio in the red sports car penetrated the night air as Stephen Woods sped through the darkness. Images from the past couple of years plagued his mind. He wasn't sure how his life had gotten to this point. He felt trapped and alone. Perhaps getting away for a few days would help him sort things out. At least that was his plan when he started this trip.

Where had things gone wrong? He and Tammy had a great life. They had been so happy, at least he had been. But he knew the answer to his own question. Working late. Business first. Home late or not at all. So Tammy waited until all the children were out of high school before she broke the news. He had never forgiven himself.

They had been together since high school and vowed they would always be together. And she had stayed right with him through college, probably putting aside her own goals although that had never been discussed. He had always been able to count on her support and now that support had been taken from him. His life had fallen apart right in front of his eyes there that night she walked out. Although he couldn't blame her and accepted full responsibility for neglecting his family and making work a first priority, he was devastated. He hadn't forgiven himself and neither had the children.

Oldest daughter, Susan, hadn't spoken to him for months after the divorce, had thrown herself into her work and broke off a six month engagement, swearing all men were pigs. Susan, strong and brilliant and immensely stubborn, their first born. Stephen was sure Susan would climb the corporate ladder with her knowledge and determination. Lindy, on the other hand, had immediately left on a Caribbean cruise after the separation which was her answer to all of life's problems. Beautiful, kind Lindy who had dropped out of college to engage in her own lavish lifestyle on Daddy's money, of course. Stephen worried that Lindy would never be serious about life or her future. Only son and third child, Cliff, became a recluse after the split, refusing to side with mother or father. Stephen was ruthless in his quest to succeed and get ahead and Stephen worried about his son's methods of furthering his career. Youngest daughter, Candy,

7

became the wild college student, drifting from one major into another, spending a lot of time in Europe with Grandmother Hastings. Stephen had patched things up with the children as much as he could, but that took a step backwards when he brought the gorgeous and sensuous Gina home as their stepmother.

Marrying Gina probably hadn't been his smartest move. Oh, sure she was gorgeous and any man would be envious of that. His partner in the firm, Greg Carter, had warned him it was too soon, but he hadn't listened. He and Greg had been college roommates and fraternity brothers. Heck, they had both dated Tammy in college. Greg possibly knew Stephen better than any other friend, but still Stephen hadn't listened to Greg's advice. And now, in retrospect, Stephen knew that Greg had been right. It had been too soon to move on.

Tammy had been gone less than a year at that point and now a second year had gone by. And he still thought about Tammy every day even though she, too, had moved on with some guy name Raoul. What a jerk! Not right for Tammy at all. But then, there would never be another man out there Stephen would consider right for Tammy.

Stephen had met Raoul once a couple of months ago when he was in Detroit on business and had been foolish enough to contact Tammy for lunch. Raoul had invited himself to join them and that made Stephen furious. Raoul was a continental type, a playboy, and Stephen thought he was insincere about his feelings for Tammy; but when he mentioned it to her, she just brushed him aside. Why not? She probably thought Stephen was no judge of character with the decisions he'd made. But there was something amiss with Raoul, something almost sinister.

Stephen's thought jumped back to Greg and the tone their relationship had taken lately. What about Greg now? There had been a growing distance between them. And when had that begun? Was it after Tammy left or after he met Gina? Or had it started years ago when Tammy married Stephen instead of Greg? Sometimes things got blurred in Stephen's memory. College. Fraternity brothers and all. Closer than a brother...'til recently. There had been more business disagreements between them in the last couple of years than there had been in their entire lives. Only last week they had ended up in a shouting match during a meeting in Greg's office.

He'd left the highway hours ago and the gravel road was not kind to the sports car. Slowing to a more reasonable speed seemed prudent at this time. His eyes strained to see the road as the two headlights spread an eerie glow across the road and pierced the blackness of night. Clearly there was no one else around and that was good. Stephen Woods needed to be alone with his thoughts.

———————●◉●———————

Tammy stood before the mirror in her bathroom, gazing at the person who had once been filled with happiness. Now she felt the most she could hope for was contentment with her life. She dabbed at her face with makeup and ran the towel through her wet hair once more and then started combing it out. This is what her life had become. Quietness. Silence she thought she would enjoy, but silence she had learned to hate. She couldn't remember how she had gotten involved with Raoul, but he had been there for her, to take her to dinner at a fancy restaurant and spoil her with lavish gifts. And she knew what he expected in return. She just wasn't ready to rush into that kind of relationship. Not after Stephen. Stephen! Quite possibly she would never get past her love for him. But she just couldn't be ignored any longer. She couldn't play second fiddle to the business. Not anymore. The children were growing up and had their own lives and Tammy had found herself alone and lonely.

And besides, Stephen hadn't wasted any time in remarrying. Perhaps her relationship with Raoul had happened in response to Stephen and Gina. But Tammy Woods had no intentions of marrying and maybe it was time Raoul was made aware of her feelings. Tonight? Or was tonight just about trying to forget?

Glancing at her watch, she realized she would be late for her engagement with Raoul if she didn't hurry. And Raoul did not like to be kept waiting. She was slipping into her shoes when the doorbell rang.

"I'm just about ready," she said as she opened the door, noticing Raoul's driver standing next to the car.

Raoul was cross.

"I do not like to be kept waiting," he barked.

"I'm sorry," she apologized. "Earrings and my bag and I will be ready to go."

It wasn't a huge request, but it seemed to irritate Raoul. Tammy had witnessed his temper before and chose to ignore it tonight. She wanted to get out a bit and Raoul was her ticket to do so. She would deal with her own emotions later.

"Ready," she said with a smile as she turned the lock on the door.

Raoul only grunted.

Chapter 2

Supper was spaghetti... again. Meatless spaghetti no less, but there was plenty of it so he shouldn't complain. Ma was doing the best she could. They all were. What was best about suppertime was the fact they were all together...Ma, Midge, Nash and Tony. And the conversation was always lively as they each shared things about their day...Midge with stories of ladies buying expensive dresses at the dress shop and always insisting they were incorrectly sized; Ma relaying the local gossip from the neighborhood or the church; and Tony telling of incidents from school and soccer practice. All in all, Nash found suppertime a time of family comfort. But today he had something to share as well.

"I got a new client today," he announced.

"That's great, Nash," Midge bubbled.

"Good for you," Ma encouraged.

"Rich, I hope," Tony added.

"Oh, she's rich alright," Nash continued. "Didn't even ask me how much. Gave me a check bigger than what I would have charged. And said there was more where that came from."

"She, huh?" Tony was interested in nudging his big brother.

"Yeah, oh, definitely a she."

"Look at that, Ma," Tony noticed his brother's inflections. "He's blushing. Nash is actually blushing."

Nash desperately tried to cover up the flush of heat he felt in his neck and face.

"Am not," he denied.

"Is, too. You see it, don't you Midgee?"

Midge, realizing her older brother was indeed sensitive, tried to dissuade the younger brother.

"Who cares? He or she. I'm so glad you've got a case to work on, Nash. What kind of case is it?"

Nash cleared his throat and was thankful to his little sister for changing the direction of the conversation.

"Missing person. Her husband," he shot a look at Tony as he emphasized the word, "is missing and she would like for me to do some investigating."

"Aw, shucks," Tony expressed his disappointment. "I was hoping this woman was available. Well, hey, if you can't find her husband, maybe she will be available."

Nash made a dive for his little brother who dodged his attempt.

"I think we'd better get out there and start mowing grass," Nash suggested. "Seems as though you still have way too much energy that needs worked off."

Grabbing caps from the hook near the back door, Tony put his on his own head and flung Nash's cap at him and the two went outside to tackle the yard work. Midge and Ma cleared the supper dishes and cleaned up the kitchen together.

"Nash's a good boy," Ma mused.

"The best brother a girl could have," Midge agreed.

Ma realized the strain that had been put on her oldest son with the passing of Pop.

"He's dedicated, always trying to provide for us," she said gratefully. "But I worry about him."

"Nash's okay, Mom," Midge comforted. "He'll be okay...and sounds like he's really interested in this new case he's working on."

Ma nodded her head as she wiped and put away the last of the dishes.

Nash hadn't been in this section of town in years. He and his buddies had come over this way once looking for some girl when they had been in high school. There was a reason he didn't explore this part of town. This is where the more affluent people lived, the people who owned big houses and fancy cars and talked about profits and losses and played golf and tennis in their spare time. And they had lots of spare time. Leisure living. That's what it was called. These people never worried about making the rent every month or ate spaghetti on a regular basis unless they chose to.

He read the street signs until he saw Hickory Lane and then turned his car to the east. Well-groomed lawns with flowering trees and spring flowers and fountains and concrete driveways and houses with wide porches on them and balconies and three car garages were impressive. Finally he slowed his car as he approached the house he was looking for. He sat for a few minutes at the side of the street contemplating what he might encounter. It was probably best he park his '85 Chevy with the dent in the passenger door somewhere on the street rather than in the driveway next to the Mercedes or the fancy sports car. Opening the door, clearly aware of the creaking noise it made, he crossed the street and started up the driveway at 2003 Hickory Lane.

It was impressive with its evergreen trees and three stories of light colored brick and the four magnificent pillars that seemed to stretch forever. And was that a four car garage or five? He was more than uncomfortable as he stood at the front door ringing the doorbell. And now he wondered if his tan slacks and polo shirt were impressive enough for this visit.

Chimes from the doorbell were answered by a rather dignified man who stood waiting for Nash to announce his reason for the visit. Probably the butler.

"Nash Adams," he stated. "Gina...er, Mrs. Woods is expecting me."

"Around to the side," the butler gestured. "Madam is in the pool area."

"Thanks," Nash said as he turned to make his way up the driveway to the rear of the house.

Water from a kidney shaped pool sparkled in the sun and Nash squinted in its brightness. When he finally was able to focus his eyes, he saw her there in a lounge chair. Pink bathing suit and long slender legs stretched out for what seemed to be miles. Sunglasses concealed her blue eyes, but the smile was still there, this time framed in hot pink.

Nash cleared his throat.

"Mrs. Woods?" he began.

She turned his direction; and taking off her sunglasses she smiled, apparently not at all surprised by his unannounced visit.

"Oh, please, Nash, call me Gina."

Oh, yes, he could call her Gina. That would be wonderful.

He smiled.

"I want you to meet my stepdaughter," she said gesturing towards the lounge next to her. "Candy, this is Nash Adams. He is going to help us locate your father."

It was only then that Nash noticed a second gorgeous woman. This one was much younger, wearing a two-piece yellow suit. Auburn hair was pulled back into a ponytail and freckles dotted her nose.

"Hi," she murmured.

"Hello."

"Don't be so formal, Nash," Gina encouraged. "Come sit down. Do you swim? I'm sure there would be a suit to fit you in the bath house."

"Oh, no, no," he regained his confidence. "I'm not here on a social call."

"Of course," Gina answered, taking a cover up from her chair and standing to put it around her bathing suit.

How did she manage to be so tan so early in the season?

Removing a small notebook and pencil from his pocket, he attempted to focus on his questions.

"So I take it you are not the first Mrs. Woods?" he said, gesturing towards Candy.

"No, Stephen and I have been married for two years now."

Only two years? Practically newlyweds.

Part of being a personal investigator is being aware of body language. And Nash did not overlook Candy's expression. He would talk to her later. Right now he was focused on Gina Woods. And that was not difficult to do.

"I have some questions," Nash struggled to proceed.

"Of course," Gina agreed. "Anything you ask."

Nash questioned her eagerness to comply. Well, she had after all been the one who had contacted him for his help.

"Do you have a recent photo of Stephen? Is the first Mrs. Woods still around?"

Candy rose from her tanning place.

"I'll get a picture for you," she said as she started towards the house. "And, yes, my mother is very much alive and lives in a suburb of Detroit."

Nash made notes.

He watched the lithe Candy as she glided towards the house.

"She is a beauty," Gina commented, noticing Nash's interest.

"Oh...uh...er, I guess," he stumbled.

"She looks a lot like her father...her coloring and all. Candy and I have become good friends. It's not the easiest thing to be the wicked stepmother."

She smiled at what she considered to be a joke at her own expense.

Nash concentrated on his notebook.

"When Stephen and I were first married, I think the children resented me...at least Candy and her sisters."

"How many children are there?"

"Stephen has three daughters and one son. The girls... Susan, Lindy and Candy. Candy is the youngest. Cliff is second to the youngest, the only son."

She paused.

Anticipating his next question, she continued.

"I do not have any children of my own."

She paused briefly and Nash felt as if that was a sad part of Gina's life. Then, apparently pushing past that thought, she continued with her usual perkiness.

"And, although the girls and I have had our issues, I really have a good relationship with their mother, Tammy."

"And you say no one has seen or heard from him the last forty-eight hours?" he asked.

"That's right. He's not answering his cell phone and the phones at the vacation houses are all turned off. All of the children are coming home. Candy lives the closest, well, here and...at Bennington College except for the time she spends with her grandmother in Europe. And Cliff lives here as well. Susan and Lindy will be here by nightfall. You'll probably want to meet them. Can you come back...let's say about 8 this evening? It will give you a chance to get a feel for the family dynamics."

"Sure," he stuttered, wishing he was more in control of the conversation. "Sure. I can do that."

At that time, his attention was drawn to the beautiful Candy who was returning from the house with a picture of her father. Of interest was the fact she chose one that had both her parents in it...Stephen Woods and his first wife, Tammy. One thing was for sure, Stephen

Woods sure knew how to surround himself with beautiful women. Tammy Woods was a looker as well.

"I wrote my mother's telephone number and address on the back of the photo," Candy said. "I'm sure my mother will be more than happy to cooperate with you."

Was that a noticeably glaring look at the second Mrs. Woods? Perhaps some resentment still lingered between Candy and her stepmother.

"Are you sure you can't join us for a swim?" Gina said as she dropped the wrap to once more expose the pink bathing suit. "It's quite warm."

Although he did in fact feel the heat and would relish a dip in the cool water, he composed himself.

"Oh, no, thank you. I must be going."

"Suit yourself," she smiled as she dove into the pool with such grace that she seemed to part the waters without even disturbing them.

"Really!" Candy said with disgust.

Nash turned from his momentary trance and noted Candy's reaction to her stepmother.

Gina surfaced from the water and waved to him before she started a backstroke across the pool.

"See you about eightish!" she called.

He stood, once again mesmerized by Gina Woods.

"See you about eightish!" Candy mimicked.

"Oh, yeah," Nash stammered. "About eight."

Nash folded his small notebook; and putting his pencil back in his pocket, started down the concrete driveway just as a second Mercedes wheeled in from the street. A beautiful blonde girl with short hair emerged from the driver's seat, one sleek long leg at a time. Were all the women in this family drop dead gorgeous? Nash nodded to her. He would obviously be introduced to her on his return visit.

———————————◦●◦———————————

Danger lurked in the seclusion of the trees along County Road 3...the gravel road that led to the cabin, danger waiting for the opportunity to pounce. It shouldn't be long now until the red sports car would come into view and then the plan could be put into motion. Someone could have been hired to take care of this matter, but this was personal. The mere thought caused an already rapid heartbeat to quicken and a bead of perspiration to break out on the forehead. Tonight would be the night. Timing was perfect.

———————●●●———————

Nash's first stop was the precinct. Louie was a couple of years older than Nash, but they had competed on the same cross-country team in high school. Louie's father and uncle had both served as cops until Louie's dad had been killed in the line of duty. Louie was working a desk in the back corner of the crowded room. File folders of cases were stacked chin high on the edge of the desk. Well, at least someone had a good amount of work.

"You got a couple of minutes?" he asked.

Louie looked up from the sheaf of papers spread across his desk.

"Hey, Nash," he greeted as he extended his hand. "Always good to see you. What's up?"

"I got a case," he began. "Just wondered if there was anything here I should know."

"You got a name?" Louie asked as his fingers started pecking on the computer.

"Yeah...a Stephen Woods. Missing for forty-eight hours. His wife came in yesterday to ask for my help."

Louie scanned the screen before him.

"Not much here. Wife reported him missing. Age 48. Executive for the Nelson Corporation: Woods & Carter Division. Pretty well to do. Don't think money was an issue...unless it was from having too much of it. Didn't show up for work on Monday. No one has heard from him. Isn't answering his cell. No clues here. No John Doe matching his description."

He pushed back from the screen and desk.

"Have at it," he encouraged. "I'll just sit here with nothing to do."

His sarcasm didn't go unnoticed as he gestured towards the stack of file folders.

"Thanks. Not much to go on," Nash replied.

Louie turned back to his desk full of papers.

"Keep in touch, Nash. Let me know if you turn up anything."

"Yeah, thanks."

Nash was out the door of the precinct and back to the office to do some serious thinking before he kept his 8 o'clock appointment with the Woods family.

———————◦●◦———————

Horace, the butler, led a very uncomfortable Nash into the foyer and walked him across the tile flooring to the plush carpeting of the formal dining room.

"Ms. Woods, Mr. Adams is here," he announced.

Gina turned with a look of anticipation on her face.

"Come in, Nash," she said as she got to her feet and extended her hand. "Come meet the rest of the family."

Nash struggled to ignore the yards of filmy green fabric that fell loosely over her body. Putting her hand in his arm, she led him to the end of the table where she offered him a seat while she continued her introductions.

"Here to your right is Cliff and you've already met Candy. On the other side of the table are Susan and Lindy."

Nash recognized Lindy as the tall blonde with the legs who he'd observed earlier driving the Mercedes. He nodded to each person as they were introduced.

"Gina thinks a private eye can find out more than the police department," Candy intentionally audibly whispered to Cliff.

Nash cleared his throat.

"Sometimes a personal detective can go places a police officer can't," he said quietly.

"You'll have to forgive my little sister," Cliff attempted to explain. "She doesn't trust anyone and isn't mature enough to make intelligent decisions."

To that, Candy punched Cliff's arm.

"Says you! Look who's talking," she pouted.

Nash smiled a bit and nodded.

"I have a younger sister, too," he said. "I understand."

Cliff smiled and Candy rolled her eyes at Nash's comment.

With a lull in the conversation, Susan, the oldest Woods' girl, spoke up.

"It's not unusual for father to be gone for a couple of days," she said. "Perhaps if he had spent more time at home..."

There was the bitterness, but only briefly did it surface. She continued.

"But it is unusual for him to be without communication. And yet, none of us has been able to contact him."

"Well, the rest of us don't hound him to death like you do," Cliff was quick to attack his older sister. "Of course you have more time than we do since you gave up men entirely."

"Don't be so hard on her, Cliff," Candy defended. "She can't help herself. Since mom's been gone, she thinks she's the woman in charge."

A bit of sarcasm?

Gina cleared her throat.

"Oh," Candy feigned apology. "I forgot. Our new mother is in charge now."

Definite sarcasm there.

"Besides, Cliff, you should talk."

Susan was back in the conversation.

"You haven't even spoken to Dad since he married Gina," she continued.

"That's none of your business," Cliff spouted back.

"But it is my business what you do in the company. And Dad's, too. I doubt that he's aware of all your business dealings. Or has he caught you red handed?"

"Nothing to catch, sister, dear. Honestly, Susan, you are the most suspicious woman I know. You're just angry because Dad didn't take you into the firm. No wonder he can't be found. Has probably had enough of your..."

"Children! Children!" Gina interrupted. "Please have a little respect for your father."

"Oh, yeah," Candy spouted. "Like you're the innocent one. You've probably done away with him so you can have all his money."

"Like you do without anything you want," Cliff attacked his little sister. "Maybe you're angry because Dad cut your allowance when he found out about all your partying."

Feeling the need to quench the rising tempers, Nash spoke up.

"So I understand that everyone around this table has made an effort to contact him without any results?"

They all concurred.

And they further agreed that Stephen Woods was not an emotional person who would do anything drastic. And, as far as they knew, he had no problems of any kind, certainly not financial. He had just chosen this time in his life to disappear in his new sports car. And of course none of them admitted to adding any stress to Stephen Woods' personal life, a fact Nash was beginning to doubt.

After more questioning and conversation, Nash excused himself from the Woods' family dinner and made his way back to the tiny office above the deli where he took out his notebook and a pad of paper and began to write, his head still whirling with the discussion he'd heard. It seemed as if everyone wanted to blame everyone else for Stephen Woods' disappearance.

Late model red sports car and license plate number were written at the top of his page.

From there, he began to analyze his thoughts about each member of the family.

Gina Woods, wife of the missing man. A beauty. Second wife. Loyal? He wondered about that. Surely a woman that beautiful could have had her choice in men. But she chose an older man with a family. Either some degree of love or; if Candy had been right in her outburst, an interest in his money. It certainly was a possibility. Gina may have pretended a good relationship with Stephen's children, but Nash doubted the truth of that from the conversation he had witnessed at the house.

Susan Woods, oldest daughter of the missing man. Quiet. Certainly not homely, but not flashy like the other two girls. Kept her hair in a pageboy cut. Wore sensible clothes. Worked in management at a large corporation. Graduated college with honors. She seemed to tolerate her stepmother, but Nash sensed real animosity there. Still, being the oldest, Susan must feel some responsibility to keep the family stable. He sensed that family was all important to Susan Woods.

Lindy Woods, middle daughter of the missing man, drove the Mercedes. Long legged beauty with short blonde hair and blue eyes. From what he could ascertain, she jetted around the world, viewing it as her playground while she spent Daddy's money. Dropped out of college to do her own thing. Probably Lindy Woods never had a thought about the relationship between her father and his young wife. She was too busy playing tennis and sipping cocktails. No, Lindy wasn't the kind of girl to get upset about life unless it stood in her way of having a lavish good time.

Cliff Woods, only son of Stephen Woods. Light brown curly hair with steel gray eyes. Recently graduated from college and worked in investments. Smart, but Nash sensed that along with the intelligence he possessed some slyness. Susan's comment about his interest in the firm did not go unnoticed. He imagined Cliff Woods could appear to fit in nicely with just about anyone if he thought he could turn it into his own advantage. And that included his relationship with his stepmother. Nash noted that Cliff more or less ignored the fact that Gina Woods was in the house. Was that intentional? Was he covering up something?

Candy Woods, youngest daughter of the missing man. Auburn hair and wide blue eyes like her father. Immature. Impressionable. Opinionated. Skeptical of Nash and the proceedings. Perhaps a bit wild. From what Nash could tell, Candy respected her older sister's opinions, but considered Susan to be rather stuffy and boring. She protected Lindy, possibly considering her to be a bit dimwitted. And although they argued, Cliff was the brother who could do no wrong. Her dislike for her stepmother peeked out from time to time from beyond the mask of pretense, but mostly it was concealed so it would work to Candy's advantage.

Indeed all the Woods' children seemed to have their own angle in this situation. Nash sensed no love or respect from any of the children towards stepmother Gina. Susan was the only one who hadn't acted favorably to Nash's questions about their biological mother. He also sensed some animosity between the children themselves. Clearly something was amiss in the Woods family.

On his way out, he noticed a light in the office next to his. He thought about stopping to introduce himself and then decided against it.

Tomorrow morning he would start placing phone calls to see what he could find out about the beach house in Alabama and the cottage in the east.

The cell phone continued to ring but his body remained still. Blood oozed from underneath him and pooled beside him.

"You have reached Stephen Woods. You know what to do. Name, number and brief message."

"Daddy, are you there?" the voice begged. "Pick up if you can hear me. We are worried about you and need to hear from you."

The battery on the phone had received all the messages it could and fell silent.

Chapter 3

If there was one thing Nash Adams had learned early in his career, it was to have good contacts in all parts of the country. By 10 the following morning, he had accessed his network of people and had an answer from the cottage in the east. He knew a guy who knew a guy who knew the caretakers of the cottage property. At Nash's request, they had gone out to the cottage and looked around. All was as it should be. No sign of Stephen Woods or anyone else having been there; and according to the caretaker, the place had been closed up since some time last fall.

The beach house was much the same story. Mr. Woods had not been to the beach house nor had anyone else from the Woods' family. It had not been used since last August when Candy Woods and a group of her college friends had spent a week there partying. The caretaker remembered it well because of the three times the police were called in to settle complaints from nearby neighbors.

That left the cabin in Colorado and Nash Adams had no contacts in that area. He called the local police station but no one there had reported any suspicious activity. No record of any red sports car on their screen. They weren't quite sure of the location of the cabin and a huge case was underway in their small town and they were a little shorthanded at the time and couldn't spare any manpower to investigate such a vague request.

Nash quickly packed an overnight bag and was walking into the airport terminal less than an hour later. It was late by the time he arrived and the plane had to circle the airport several times due to dense fog before it could land so he rented a car and found a cheap motel close by; and after a call to Ma to let her know he was okay, he turned in for a peaceful night's sleep.

He was awakened by the sound of the motel alarm clock going off at 4 am. He hadn't set it. Some other traveler must have thought that was an amusing trick to play on the next guest. It wasn't. Try as he may, he couldn't go back to sleep. Information floated in and out of his head and he tossed from one side of the bed to the other until he finally decided the best course of action was just to get up since he wasn't sleeping anyway. He let the steam from the shower wash over him and release the stress of the late night flight.

The smell of bacon and eggs at the corner diner reminded him how hungry he was. It also gave him an opportunity to ask a few discreet questions of the waitress. He showed her a picture of Stephen Woods and asked if she had seen anyone resembling him in the past few days. She had been off work for a couple of days, but perhaps Edna would have remembered. He was in luck. Edna was a portly woman with thick glasses, but Nash surmised not a lot got past her in the diner or in the little town. Yes, she believed she had seen the man the day before yesterday. She remembered him because of the unique color of his hair. Yes, Nash remembered, Gina had said Candy's coloring was like her father's. Auburn hair. No, the man with the auburn hair hadn't divulged any information about why he was in town or where he was going. But he had eaten breakfast there and asked for a sandwich to go. Ham and cheese, as she remembered.

"Call me if you remember anything else," Nash said as he placed his calling card into her hand.

Edna agreed and was still holding Nash's calling card in her hand when she observed him getting into the rental car and driving away. Tucking the card in her apron pocket, she continued serving coffee to the breakfast crowd.

It was a little past nine when Nash and the rental car left town on Route 3. With Cliff's sketchy map in his hands, he contemplated his next move just in case he came up dry on this location as well as he had on the other two. Thoughts of finding Stephen Woods and convincing him his family was worried about his absence and needed him to return flitted through his mind. Yes, he could wrap this case up quickly and collect his fee and that would be the end of it. Along with those thoughts came the images of the Woods' women dancing in his head...red lips, long legs, beauty beyond compare.

Although Route 3 was a paved road, he was in the foothills before he realized it and the road rapidly began to twist and turn. His focus surely needed to be on his driving. The morning skies grew dark and threatened a storm as the headlights of the car cast a short beam across the road. He had just passed the sign that said the county road he was to take was three miles ahead when the cloud burst broke loose. Kicking the wipers into high speed, he slowed the car and strained to see the road ahead of him. Thunder rumbled and groaned while lightning streaked across the purple sky. It was only by sheer luck that lightning chose to reveal the turn off sign. He wheeled the car to the right and immediately felt the dirt and gravel attack the tires of the rental. This would be slow going. That's okay. He was in no hurry.

Twice he thought he had lost sight of the road and would end up in a ditch. He didn't relish that so he crept along the road, hoping there wouldn't be any wash outs along the way. A deer suddenly darting across in front of him caused him to jerk the wheel. He felt the back tires lose traction and he gently pressed the gas pedal and prayed. Luckily the tires were able to keep moving in what now had become mostly mud.

A deer should not have surprised him. After all, wasn't this a hunting cabin he was trying to find? Of course there would be deer and other assorted animals in this densely wooded area.

What was this? Was the road just completely stopping before him? He certainly hoped he wouldn't have to hike in this weather. He sat patiently for a few moments; and as the rain let up a bit, he saw faint tire tracks bearing towards the right and the outline of a building at the end of them. And over to the far left, partially hidden in a grove of trees, he saw the red sports car. Surely this then was his destination. Pulling a photo of the cabin from a manila envelope and comparing that to what he could see, he was convinced this indeed was the Woods' cabin. It appeared to be deserted. If Stephen Woods had come here to enjoy nature, he quite possibly was out hunting or walking. Probably another dead end. Waiting for a lull in the rain, he chose just the right moment to run. Reaching the safety of the cabin porch just as another deluge burst forth, he attempted to scrape the mud from his shoes on the top step of the porch.

Standing for a brief moment, he took time to peer into the darkness, half way expecting something or someone to emerge from the woods while his body shivered from the chill of the spring rain.

The screen door rattled, but no answer came in response to his knock on the door.

Where had Gina said they kept the spare key? He fumbled until he found the ledge of the window and felt for the small box. None there. He felt for the other side of the door where he found the second window ledge and a flash of lightning revealed a small weathered box near one corner. Grasping the box, he opened it and found the key. Making his way back to the door, he felt for the keyhole and hoped for another flash of lightning which did not come. Finally the key sunk into the hole; and turning it, the door creaked open.

A unique and repulsive odor quickly filled his nostrils as he searched for a light switch. No electricity. While making his way to what he thought was a table in front of a side window, his foot stumbled against an object on the floor. Reaching for the lighter in his pocket and flipping it, he was met with the eerie sight of the body. Immediately the breakfast he'd had a few hours earlier began to churn in his stomach. Struggling to keep his nose from inhaling, he turned to find a kerosene lamp on the table and lit it with the lighter. The scene was no better no matter when light was shone on it. He couldn't miss the auburn hair. Nash had found Stephen Woods.

Stepping onto the porch and feeling the coolness of the rain wash over his body, he reached for his cell phone and dialed the emergency number. Then he waited. He did not want to disturb the crime scene.

Chapter 4

An anxious Nash nervously waited for the local police to answer his 911 call. Rain ceased and the sun broke through the clouds, clearing the atmosphere. His lungs craved fresh air. He would wait until after the police showed up before he placed a call to Gina Woods.

Since the rain had let up, he walked to the red sports car. Open. Keys still in it. Evidently the car was of no value to the attacker. Checking the glove box only revealed the car was registered to Stephen Woods and the insurance was up to date. One untouched ham and cheese sandwich lay on the seat. Otherwise the car was clean. Overnight and computer bags still in the trunk. Apparently Stephen Woods had been accosted before he had a chance to unpack.

Nash's next call was to Louie back home at the police department.

"Louie here," he heard the voice.

Nash swallowed hard.

"Anyone there?" came the question.

"Yeah, I'm here," Nash choked.

"Is that you, Nash? You sound funny like you're a million miles away."

"Not quite that far," Nash confessed. "Just as far as Colorado."

"What are you doin' out there, man?"

"Working a case."

"Oh, yeah, I remember. The missing person," Louie remembered. "How's that going?"

Nash paused.

"It's not a missing person anymore," he fumbled. "It's a murder case."

He had Louie's attention.

"Wow! Talk to me."

"I just got here to the scene and saw the body and called the locals."

"Good. Good. That's the right thing to do. You okay?"

"Yeah, yeah. I'm okay. Just hadn't expected to find this."

"Can I do anything from here?"

"Not that I know of. I've got to call Gi...Mrs. Woods."

"Want me to do that?" Louie offered.

"No, no," Nash said softly. "Something I think I should do myself."

"Okay if you say so. But I'll be here if you need me."

"Thanks man. Just wanted you to know. I'll see you when I get back."

Flashing lights coming up the lane had Nash's attention. Two uniformed officers, weapons drawn, opened the door of the squad car and approached him. He raised his hands in response.

"What's going on here?" the older of the two asked.

"I believe there's been a crime committed here," Nash attempted to explain.

"What kind of a crime?"

"A murder."

"Who are you?"

"My name is Nash Adams. I'm a private detective. I was on a case and this is what I found. I called you guys as soon as I saw the body. Nothing's been disturbed."

"Let's see some identification."

Chase cautiously began to move his arms down.

"I'm reaching for my wallet, okay?" he said.

The older officer motioned to the younger one to take the wallet from Nash's hand.

"He's who he says he is," the younger officer confirmed.

Nodding, the older officer seemed to think it was okay for them to holster their weapons. He stepped to the doorway to view the scene.

Upon closer inspection, he murmured, "Yep, looks like a murder to me."

Nash stifled his sarcastic comments and turned his attention to the phone call he dreaded to make. He waited nervously while Gina's phone rang. And then the lyrical sound of her voice.

"Hello," she chirped.

"This is Nash Adams," he said, attempting to clear his suddenly foggy voice.

"Nash, how good to hear from you. Have you located anything about Stephen?"

He swallowed hard.

"Mrs. Woods…Gina, are you alone?"

"No. As a matter of fact, Cliff is here with me right now."

"Good," Nash responded. "Gina, you had better sit down."

"Why?" he could hear the panic raise in her voice. "What are you trying to say?"

"Stephen is dead," he said bluntly.

There seemed to be no better way to break the news.

There was a silence on the other end of the phone.

"Gina…Gina, are you there?"

After another silence, a male voice came on the line.

"This is Cliff Woods," he said in a business-like manner. "Who's this?"

"Hello, Cliff. This is Nash Adams. I'm calling from the hunting cabin in Colorado. I've located your father. It appears he has been shot. He's dead."

Thoughts of being told of his own father's death just a few short months ago surfaced in Nash's head. He swallowed hard, trying to find more words. None seemed adequate.

After a few more minutes of uncomfortable silence, Cliff resumed the conversation asking for the details and thanking Nash for his efforts.

"I'll start making arrangements on this end," Cliff said, attempting to steady his voice. "I appreciate anything you can do out there. I'll be in touch."

"Glad to help you in any way I can," Nash was genuine.

Then Gina Woods wanted to talk again.

"Thank you, Nash," she sniffled. "Thank you for finding Stephen."

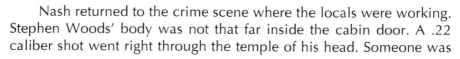

Nash returned to the crime scene where the locals were working. Stephen Woods' body was not that far inside the cabin door. A .22 caliber shot went right through the temple of his head. Someone was very lucky or a pretty good shot. Stephen had to have been standing at the cabin door, facing out when the bullet entered. That also meant that someone had probably checked his handiwork before he closed and locked the cabin door.

The door was being checked for fingerprints and the grounds were being scoured for footprints or other signs. Nash walked the perimeter of the cabin as well; and then, with the younger of the two officers, fanned out farther into the woods, hoping to find some clue.

"Over here," he shouted.

The young officer came running with his pistol drawn.

"There are broken twigs from these shrubs," Nash said. "And look, here where the grass is matted down."

"Be careful where you walk. Perhaps we can find a footprint."

None was found, possibly because of the morning's downpour of rain.

"Sure looks like someone was waitin' here for some time," the officer added as he examined fast food containers.

They looked around and the officer found an empty cartridge which he promptly bagged. Nash was impressed with his thoroughness.

No other clues were discovered. With the assurance that a full report would be sent to Louie, Nash stayed the rest of the afternoon to help make the arrangements as he has promised Cliff and then caught a late flight back home.

Chapter 5

———————•●•———————

It was a nice day for a funeral, Nash mused. Well, no day was a nice day for a funeral, but the weather had cooled again which was going to make standing out in the hot sun a bit more tolerable. Nash had never been to this cemetery before. Any funeral he had ever attended had been on the other side of town. This one reeked of wealth with its stones all standing straight, reaching for the sky. Everything was well groomed and formal. The cemetery that held Pop Adams' remains had a variety of decorations according to each family's personal taste and some of the stones had settled with time and listed to one side. But there was a feeling of comfort when he visited there, not the coldness he felt here. He stood towards the edge of the assembled group of mourners, observing the scene as it played out before him. He had never seen so much black worn in so many different ways.

Of course Gina was the first to attract his attention. Or perhaps it was the red rose she carried that caused him to notice her. She wore a black sheath dress with a v neckline exposing her already tanned shoulders and her bare arms. One arm was lined with black and silver bracelets. The length of the dress was just right for showing off her gorgeous legs or was it the black straps of her sandals that claimed that position? A wide brimmed hat and dark glasses pretty well hid her face except for the lips outlined in red lipstick.

Interesting enough, Cliff was assisting his stepmother. The stark whiteness of his shirt stood out against his black pinstriped suit. Every light brown hair on his head was immaculately in place. Looking good enough to have stepped out of a fashion shoot, he graciously held a chair at the far right of the row for Gina and then stood behind her.

No surprise that the eldest daughter wore a black pant outfit with a short fitted jacket, perhaps not willing to give up her business like aura. She wore no hat or gloves, a pair of low heels and no sunglasses. She chose to sit in chair number four of the five that were there, leaving a distinct gap between her and stepmother Gina.

Lindy Woods looked stunning with her short blonde hair and its windblown look enhanced by a small hat which formed a band over the top of her head. Her dress had a fitted sleeveless bodice covered in black sequins with a flowing skirt just long enough to allow her long legs to be of interest. Being tall, she wore a short heel. She slithered into chair number three next to her older sister. Black gloves adorned her hands and held a white handkerchief which she frequently used to dab at her eyes.

When Candy Woods made her entrance in her short black skirt and the black silky overblouse with a huge white artificial flower on one shoulder, she walked promptly to Cliff and whispered something to him. She appeared to be a bit miffed about something. She then walked around to the other end of the short row of seats next to the coffin and made an issue of moving Lindy down next to Gina so she could sit in chair number three between her two sisters. Apparently she had no intention of sitting next to her stepmother. Gina turned her head slightly as Lindy slipped into the seat beside her and stepson Cliff gave Gina's shoulder a reassuring pat.

But Nash's attention was drawn towards the next guests. A man with black hair wearing a light gray suit and tie instead of the traditional black and sporting a dark tan escorted a woman who wore a black dress with a flouncy skirt and a filmy cape type jacket that flowed over her shoulders. She also wore a wide brimmed hat attached to a black veil, completing her ensemble with black gloves and black heels. There was something in the way she moved that caused all eyes to focus on her. As she made her way to the one remaining seat, the man in the light gray suit took his position behind her. Her oldest daughter, Susan, reached over and patted her mother's arm.

The fifth and final seat then was occupied by Tammy Woods, first wife of Stephen Woods. And the man in the gray suit must have been Tammy's companion, Raoul. It was Nash's understanding that Tammy had never remarried.

Other than the faithful butler, Horace, Nash did not recognize any of the other people standing in the small group of mourners.

The minister began his remarks as the other guests paying their respects were encouraged to move closer to the mourning family members. Nash studied the beautiful floral sprays and tried to compute how much money had been spent on flowers. The casket was the most elaborate Nash had ever seen. Polished oak, he believed, trimmed with sparkling brass. Lots of sparkling brass. Nothing like the one Nash and his family had been able to afford for his father just a few short months ago.

Hearing the minister call for the remaining prayer, Nash bowed his head and gave thanks for his family and the love they shared. Differences of opinions and spats would probably always take place; but when the Adams family came around the table at suppertime, there was an undeniable bond.

Nash waited until the group began to disperse and was just about to leave himself when Gina Woods approached him. Touching his arm and giving him a slight smile, she invited him to the house for a gathering of friends and family. It seemed like a good opportunity for Nash to observe some family interaction so he accepted the offer.

Post funeral refreshments were abundant at the Woods' house and Nash stood with his plate, nibbling on vegetables and dip and cute little snacks he didn't recognize when Gina approached him.

"Thank you for all you've done, Nash," she purred.

Nash swallowed the last of a piece of carrot before he spoke.

"I wish it could have been better news," he said as he temporarily lost himself in her blue eyes.

"Of course," she said.

There was an uncomfortable silence.

"You have my heartfelt condolences," he offered.

"Thank you," she said shyly, once again gently putting her hand on his arm.

He felt the heat coming once again to his neck and face.

"If you ever need any more personal detective work," he began, "I hope you will call on me."

She seemed surprised at that remark.

"Oh, I hoped you'd stay on," she said. "The case is not solved. I want to know who killed my husband. Besides, I have a check for you on my desk in the den."

"Oh, I've already been amply paid for my services," he resisted.

"Not hardly. There was your flight to Colorado and all those things."

"I imagine the police will take over from here."

She seemed disappointed.

"I really hoped you'd continue on," she said, slightly extending her lower lip.

And did she move closer to him when she said that or did he just imagine it?

She seemed to want to change the subject.

"Have you met Tammy yet?" she asked. "Stephen's first wife?"

"No. No, I haven't."

"I believe I saw her heading for the gardens in the pool area. You might want to speak with her. Go ahead. I'll catch up with you later."

While pondering the purpose of her last phrase, he found his way to the gardens. Well, if he was going to get paid, he might as well do as much interviewing as he could.

He hadn't intended to eavesdrop on anyone's conversation, but he was too close to turn around without being seen so he stood perfectly still behind the honeysuckle vines growing on the lattice.

"How could you be so rude?"

"Tammy, I've given you plenty of time to get over him."

"I am over him," she shouted. "I divorced him, didn't I?"

"Oh, yeah, that you did," the man in the gray suit said angrily. "You divorced him on paper but you never gave up on him."

"You just don't understand, Raoul. We had the children..."

"You bet I do," he replied. "I understand everything about you. How many times have I asked you to marry me? And how many times have you refused? Every time, that's how many! You say you care for me, but he's always between us."

"You're being unreasonable. This is a really traumatic time for the children...and yes, for me. Now then, I've said it. Are you satisfied?"

"No. Not until you change how you feel about him."

"For heaven's sake, you're speaking of the dead now, Raoul. Show a little respect."

"Maybe now that he's dead, you will concentrate on me...on us."

"You make it sound like you're glad he's dead," she spit at him.

"You figure it out, Tammy," Raoul shouted.

Nash did not hear her reply, but thought perhaps she had started to cry.

"That's it. I'm out of here," Raoul said. "Call me when you're ready to leave."

Nash waited what he thought was a respectful amount of time before he moved from his place of eavesdropping behind the honeysuckle.

"Oh, I'm sorry," he said. "I didn't realize anyone was out here."

Tammy Woods looked up at him with incredibly soulful eyes and he understood right away what Stephen Woods had seen in this woman. Pulling a handkerchief from his pocket, he offered it to her. She took it and wiped her eyes.

"Excuse me," she said. "I must be a mess."

"Not hardly," he crooned.

There was something about this woman that caused him to feel an instant connection. He wanted to take her in his arms and console her and tell her that everything would be all right.

She offered her hand.

"I'm Tammy Woods," she said softly.

"Nash Adams," he was breathless.

"Oh, you're the private detective Gina hired."

"Er...yes I am. Nash Adams."

Hadn't he just told her his name? Was he making a fool of himself?

"Well, I thank you for finding my husband," she said genuinely and then began to cry again.

He touched her shoulder.

"You certainly have four fine children," he tried to redirect the conversation.

"Thank you," she sniffled. "The girls never did forgive him, you know. I wanted so much for that to happen. They just never understood."

"You really love him, don't you?"

"I never stopped," she confessed.

"But it's my understanding that you left him."

"Yes, I did," she said, "but I didn't want to. Not really. It was just the loneliness of him being gone all the time and so involved in his work. And the children were growing up and finding their own lives."

"Do you know of anyone who would want to hurt your husband?" Nash asked.

She thought for a bit.

35

"No, not that I can think of. To the best of my knowledge, he mostly got along with everyone. Perhaps Greg would be of some help."

"Greg?"

"Yes, Greg Carter, Stephen's business partner."

"Thanks for the tip," Nash said mustering an encouraging smile.

"You've very welcome," she said as she offered his handkerchief back to him. "And thanks for the use of your handkerchief."

Taking the handkerchief from her hand, he gave her a tender touch.

"Oh, and Mr. Adams," she said, "please find my husband's murderer...please."

He was mesmerized by this woman. She was not only beautiful on the outside, but he sensed what a beautiful person existed underneath the facade.

Making his way back into the crowd, he sought out Lindy first.

"Hello, Lindy," he began. "I'm sorry about your father."

"Thank you, Mr. Adams," she replied. "Daddy was the best."

Susan overheard the remark and interjected herself into the conversation.

"Oh, Lindy, be real. You know as well as I do that you and he were always at odds over your lavish lifestyle and spending. As a matter of fact, I believe he had cut your allowance considerably. Don't imagine you were too pleased about that, were you?"

"What went on between Daddy and me is none of your business, Susan," Lindy retaliated.

"It could become Mr. Nash's business if you had some part in father's death," Susan accused.

"What a thing to say, Susan, I could never do that."

"I imagine some of your jet set friends could though. I hear some of your closest friends are in the mafia."

"Maybe you should check your information more carefully before you start accusing people."

"Yeah, I'll do that," Susan snapped.

"Yeah, just do that," Lindy retaliated.

With that, the two girls walked off in different directions, leaving Nash standing there alone. So Lindy really did have some spunk after all.

"You'll have to excuse my sisters, Nash," Cliff explained as he walked up to the bewildered Nash. "They're a little emotional today. Well, a little more than usual. You understand. You said you had a sister, right?"

Yes, Nash had a little sister who under the worst of circumstances would never behave like these girls.

He smiled instead of sharing his thoughts.

"Yeah, girls can be emotional," he agreed. "I guess stepmothers can be as well."

He watched Cliff Woods for some kind of reaction to his statement. What he saw for just a second was a bit of embarrassment which Cliff quickly covered up.

"Yes, Gina's okay," he explained. "Perhaps misunderstood a bit. The girls have made it really rough on her. Sometimes I feel sorry for her."

"Yeah, I can see that," Nash continued, ignoring but aware of the brief look of panic in Cliff's eyes. "She is a beautiful woman alright, isn't she?"

Nash gestured across the room towards Gina who was being consoled by a small group of guests.

"You'll get no argument from me on that one," Cliff admitted. "She is beautiful...and rich now," he added. "No doubt there will be a line of hungry men just waiting at the door."

"Well, she has you to protect her, right, Cliff?"

Cliff seemed to return from another place.

"Oh, yeah, right. I guess."

"Who's the man with the yellow tie talking to her now?" Nash questioned. "I noticed him at the cemetery."

Not only was the man talking to Gina Woods, but he was also offering a sympathetic shoulder for her to cry against which she seemed to be a bit anxious to use.

"Oh, that's Greg Carter, my Dad's business partner. Come on, I'll introduce you."

Nash followed Cliff through the crowd of sympathy offering acquaintances.

Greg Carter proved to be distant, not overly friendly, even to the point of being evasive. He kept Gina's hand in his and did not offer to shake hands with Nash. And Nash was pretty sure he could interpret

Mrs. Carter's look as one of contempt for her husband. He would keep watch on this scenario.

At that point, Candy, with a glass of liquor in her hand sidled up to him.

"Well, Mr. Adams," she slurred, "what do ya think of our dysfunctional family?"

She made three attempts to get the word dysfunctional out of her mouth.

"It looks like you've had a little too much to drink, Candy," Nash admonished.

"Nonsense. Don't tell me you're gonna tell me I'm a bad little girl. I hear that all the time from my bestest friends."

With that she swilled the last of the drink and reeled a bit.

"Here," Nash steadied, "you'd better sit down a while."

"I'll tell you something," she leaned closer to him as if to tell him a secret. "I know who murdered my dad."

"Really?" Nash said, desperately trying to get her into a chair without causing a scene.

"Yep."

"And who would that be?" Nash tried to humor her.

"My mom," she whispered.

Although he was a bit surprised at that revelation, he considered the source.

"And why would your mother want to kill your father?"

"Shh," she whispered. "She's still in love with him."

"Then why would she want to hurt him?"

"She doesn't want anyone else to have him...like Gina," and she shook her head as if she had stated a fact. "Yep, that's it."

"You sit right here," Nash instructed.

He quickly found Cliff.

"I think your little sister is in need of your assistance," he said.

Cliff looked around the room until he found Candy sitting in the chair.

"Yeah, she does have a problem," he sighed. "Thanks. I'll take care of it."

Spying Mrs. Carter lingering near the bar, Nash made his way towards her. Pretending to be interested in the selection of liquor, he waited until he saw Mrs. Carter's interest focus on one area of the room. Nash's eyes followed her line of vision. Gina Woods' head rested on Greg Carter's shoulder as he held her in his arms. Greg Carter was busy consoling the grieving widow.

Chapter 6

———————●◆●———————

"How's it going, Nash?" Mr. Meijer inquired as Nash made his way through the deli to the stairway that led to the second floor.

There was always a good smell in the deli, aromas of freshly baked bread and spices of luncheon meats. Mr. Meijer was working behind the counter and Mrs. Meijer was running clean wet cloths over the counters while Anne wiped down the tables and chairs where later customers would be eating sandwiches and potato salad and huge dill pickles from the glass barrel which had taken up residence on top of the meat counter.

"Not too bad," Nash replied. "Nice day out there."

"No rain?" Mr. Meijer inquired.

"Don't think so," Nash answered.

Mr. Meijer turned to his wife.

"Mama, today is the day we put tables out front. I'll get the tables and chairs. Anne, you crank down the awning."

Anne finished the last of the tables and gave Nash a shy smile as she started towards the front door and the awning.

"Let me help you," Nash offered.

Anne Meijer wore a simple dress and a button sweater over it. Anklets with her practical shoes gave her the appearance of a girl from the 1940's. The shy young lady was always so quiet, she was easy to overlook; but she was always pleasant and readily accepted his help when he held the door for her as they walked out into the morning sun.

Nash looked around and found the crank for the awning.

"How's this thing work?" he asked as he studied it.

"Oh, it's quite simple," she informed.

"Are you making fun of me?" he joked.

"Oh, no," she was flustered. "I would never do that."

"I'll bet you wouldn't," he said.

She took the crank from his hand and inserted it in the hook and started to turn.

"Hey, I think I can do that," he quipped.

She stepped aside so he could take over, being very careful to avoid any physical contact with him. Slowly the awning began to unfold.

"Be careful," she warned. "Sometimes…"

But it was too late. Accumulation of rain from yesterday's shower took the opportunity to dump and Nash stepped back to escape the deluge. Well, at least part of it. He caught a glimpse of Anne out of the corner of his eye as she attempted to cover up the smile on her lips with her hand.

"You laughin' at me?" he smiled as well.

"Oh, no," she became serious. "Oh, no, I would never laugh at you."

Clearly she was embarrassed.

"It's okay, Anne," he attempted to explain. "Sometimes people laugh together and that's okay."

She once again gave him a shy smile. Mr. Meijer arrived with the little round tables and chairs and Nash took them from him and helped him set them up under the canopy. Anne disappeared and returned with yet more wiping cloths and some fresh flowers to put in the center of each table.

"Thanks, Nash, you're a good boy," Mr. Meijer expressed his gratitude.

"No problem."

And Nash was off up the stairs to his office.

Stuffiness greeted him as he unlocked the door and he immediately crossed the room to open the one and only window in his office. As he stood there gazing into the nearly empty parking lot, he thought about Stephen Woods' case. It seemed the Woods family was quick to accuse each other of having been involved in some way with the murder. And, yet, none of them had presented any really good reason for committing the act.

Greg Carter's interest in Gina Woods might be a little too personal and that could be a possible motive. Love triangles were always messy. And that could apply to Cliff's more than casual interest in his stepmother. And just what was Cliff's interest in Gina? Could it be defined as romantic or was it just Cliff being clever enough to know that if Gina stood to inherit, he needed to remain in her good graces. And, what if Gina welcomed Cliff's attentions and did consider them romantic and made a conscious decision that she wanted the younger man?

None of the girls…Susan, Lindy or Candy…had any love for their stepmother, but to hurt their own father? For what reason? Cutting back their spending money? That hardly seemed a motive at this time. Hated him enough for causing the divorce? Umm! Probably not. However, at this time, nothing could be eliminated.

Could the inebriated Candy have stumbled onto something when she babbled that her mother killed her father because she didn't want any other woman to have him? Stranger things had happened, but Nash found it hard to believe the sensitive woman with the soft gray eyes was capable of doing such a thing.

Nash needed to know more about Raoul and what kind of a person he was. So far, the opinion wasn't too favorable. He just might need to take a trip to the Detroit area and nose around a bit. He needed to check with Louie down at the precinct to see what, if anything, had turned up there. And then he thought he would pay a visit to the offices of Woods & Carter at the Nelson Corporation.

Louie didn't have much information to share and agreed with Nash that starting with Stephen Woods' company was probably a good choice.

"Let me know if you turn up something," he said as he reached for the ringing phone.

"Will do," Nash answered.

"I'll get right on it," he heard Louie say to the person on the phone and wondered when Louie would ever find the time to decrease the number of file folders stacked at the end of his desk.

The offices of Woods & Carter were located downtown in the newly developed urban area. The Nelson Corporation building was easy to find as it was the largest, most impressive building in the area. A blend of steel and glass greeted him as he opened the front doors. After reading the directory, he entered the elevator and pushed the button for the sixth floor.

"Hold the door," he heard the voice as he reached to keep the elevator door from closing.

"What floor?" he asked.

"Sixth," she said as she clutched at an armload of papers threatening to fall.

He came to her assistance.

"Thanks," she murmured as she struggled with a wisp of dark brown hair tumbling down her forehead.

Not having a free hand, she attempted to blow it out of her face.

Nash smiled at her efforts, but the strand of hair persisted.

"Is that all homework?" he asked.

"Yes, just like high school," she sighed. "I never seem to get everything done at my desk."

"Sounds to me like you're either slow or your bosses are overworking you," he ventured.

"Well," she said freely, ignoring his remark about her being slow, "one of the big bosses was murdered last week and things have been hectic ever since. What I usually accomplish has been put aside to answer an unusual volume of telephone calls."

"That's too bad," Nash seemed sincere. "I mean too bad about your boss being killed and too bad about the extra work."

She was petite with dark brown hair cut short and deep brown eyes which smiled at him from behind a pair of dark rimmed glasses. She wore a plain navy blue skirt with sensible shoes and a silky short sleeved printed blouse that closed with a bow at the neck.

The packages she carried started to slip again.

"Here, let me help you with those," Nash offered. "I'm getting off on six as well."

She accepted his offer, the elevator door opened into a rather spacious area and Nash saw the sign for Woods & Carter with an arrow pointing towards the right on the wall across from the elevator door.

Everything smelled new on this floor. Fresh paint. New carpet. The hallways were spacious as well...not at all like the stuffy room above Meijer's deli... and Nash followed the girl down one of them to a set of glass doors clearly marked Woods & Carter which he opened for her. She approached a nearby desk; and setting her purse and lunch container on it, turned to him.

"Right here will be fine," she said. "And thank you."

Nash looked at the nameplate on the desk. Katie.

He stood for a few minutes contemplating his next move. She looked at him suspiciously.

"Oh, Katie," he stumbled, "I'd like to improve your day. How about I take you to lunch?"

Thinking that was a rather clumsy beginning, he felt awkward and thought he had blown the whole possibility.

She started to decline.

"And I can see you've already brought your lunch, but it might be helpful under the circumstances to get out of the office for a bit. Please...let me try to brighten your day."

She began to weaken.

"I'm really a nice guy," he explained. "And you seem like a really nice girl. We can eat somewhere close by if you're worried about being late getting back for work."

"She'd be glad to," an older woman said as she walked by. "She could use a distraction."

Both Nash and Katie smiled.

"Okay, I accept," Katie said. "I get off at twelve noon sharp."

"Your distraction will be here promptly at twelve noon," Nash said with enthusiasm.

He started to leave.

"Hey, I don't even know your name," she called after him.

"It's Nash," he answered as he was going through the glass doors.

Katie nervously watched the clock the rest of the morning. About eleven o'clock, Mrs. Babcock walked by her desk again.

"So," she began, "did you take the young man up on his offer to go to lunch?"

Katie immediately felt flush.

"As a matter of fact, I did," she replied.

"Good," Mrs. Babcock seemed satisfied with that answer. "Where did you meet him?"

Now Katie really did feel the redness creep up her neck.

"I met him on the elevator on my way to work this morning."

Mrs. Babcock raised her eyebrows at that particular bit of information.

"Well, sometimes we need to do something rash and different for a change. Things have been so crazy around here since the Mr.

Woods incident last week. We all need some relief and change of pace. Enjoy yourself and relax a bit, Katie."

She started to leave and then returned.

"He sure is a nice looking guy."

Katie nodded in agreement. But had she actually taken a good look at him? Would she even recognize him when he walked in the door? What she did remember was that he was tall and lean and his eyes were blue. Yes, his eyes were definitely blue. And he had a nice smile, too.

She cleared her desk by 11:50 and sat nervously anticipating his arrival. At 11:55, she opened her desk drawer and took out a pad and pencil so she could pretend to be busy and not necessarily appearing to be waiting for him. At 11:57, she felt an uneasiness in her stomach. Maybe she had made a mistake. After all, she didn't know anything about this man. True, he had been generous in helping her this morning in the elevator. Well, having lunch with him did not mean anything more than that; and if he turned out to be a creep, she'd just brush him aside. But what if he turned out to be a pervert?

Her thoughts were interrupted by the glass doors opening and there stood Nash. She forgot all about pretending to be busy when he arrived and immediately stood up and picked up her purse. Nash smiled at her awkwardness.

"Great," he smiled. "You're ready to go."

"Yes," she said weakly.

"Good. I'm starved," he said as she walked by him and he reached to open the door for her.

She liked that. At least he was getting off to a good start by being mannerly.

"You probably know this area better than I do," he began. "Any suggestions for a place to eat?"

"Yes, as a matter of fact," she replied. "There's a little mom and pop diner just over in the next block. I enjoy eating there sometimes. Not too far to walk."

It wasn't long until she realized she would really have to speed up to keep up with his long stride. Sensing that, he slowed a bit. And she realized he had made the concession for her.

"Thanks," she said. "My legs aren't very long."

He smiled and liked her openness.

They found the restaurant and he was pleased with her choice. They were seated at a table near the window. It reminded him somewhat of Mr. Meijer's deli...small, intimate, with nice people.

"Hello, Katie," the proprietor called to her.

"I thought you said you came here once in a while. Sounds like you're a regular customer."

"I like encouraging small business owners. They are the backbone of our country, you know."

Wow, he liked this. Katie had some down to earth ideas.

"Besides, they're good people."

"This reminds me of a place I know of."

She smiled thinking she had made a good choice in restaurants and perhaps a good choice in accepting Nash's invitation.

They ordered the blue plate special for the day and then settled back. It was time to get to know Katie better.

"How long have you worked for Woods and...and..." he pretended to know nothing about the company.

"Mr. Carter. He's the other partner. Well, I guess he's the only partner now...surviving partner. Anyway, I've been there three years now," she said. "Started out in the secretarial pool and then got my current job after I'd been there a few months."

"Do you like your job?"

"Oh, yes. It's just that it's been a bit hectic of late."

"I guess that's understandable. You said one of your bosses was murdered?"

"Yes. Terrible. Tragic. The entire office has been upset."

"Nice guy, huh?"

"The best. Mr. Woods was a fine man."

Here Nash saw a bit of emotion when Katie spoke of Stephen Woods.

"Did you know him well?"

"Not super well. But he was the kind of man who would stop by your desk occasionally and ask how you were doing. Things like that. He knew my name. Well, he took the time to know everyone's name...right on down to the guy who sweeps up at the end of the day. And his wife was special, too. Well, his first wife. Divorced. She used to drop by the office often and was very kind and they made such a great couple. We all hated it when they got divorced. And he was messed up with that for a long time. I don't know what happened to cause the break up."

"And Mr. Carter? Is that his name? I take it he's not the same kind of boss."

"You think right. He seems nice enough, but not personable with the staff, not approachable."

She looked around cautiously.

"But don't tell anyone I said that. I shouldn't have said that at all."

"No problem," Nash said calmly. "Your comments are safe with me."

"Mr. Carter was out of the office for a several days when we got the news about Mr. Woods. We all felt like we were just adrift for a time. And then he was pretty upset when he came back. It was a very trying time."

Nash needed to be cautious about asking too many questions and arousing suspicion. But there were many more questions he wanted to ask.

"Oh, here's our meal," Katie announced. "They are very good about quick delivery. Most everyone who eats here works somewhere close by."

It was home cooked food much like Nash's mother would prepare and it was good. Conversation was good. Nash studied Katie from across the table. Nice looking girl. Intelligent. Katie noticed he'd stopped eating.

"You'd better eat up," she said, gesturing towards his plate. "Lunch hour is just that. No more."

He smiled and scooped up another forkful of mashed potatoes.

"How about you?" she asked.

"What about me?"

"Well, you know what I do for a living. How about you?"

Nash thought a minute, taking time for a swallow of water. He really wasn't ready to share the information that he was in the private detective business.

"I'm in business for myself. Just getting started. Had to drop out of college. My pop passed away and I needed to help out with expenses."

She appeared to accept that.

"Yeah, I am helping out my mother as well. Plus a little brother who's still in high school."

"Wow, we have some things in common. I have a little brother who's still in high school as well."

"Small world, huh?"

They finished their meal and she checked her watch.

"Time to go?" he asked.

"A few more minutes," she answered. "We could walk back by way of the park if you'd like."

He liked that. She had suggestions.

"Good idea," he agreed.

It was a pleasant walk in the park. He learned she was twenty one years old, still lived at home helping out her widowed mother and little brother. She liked baseball and picnics and he didn't think she had a boyfriend. But it was coming up one o'clock and she needed to get back to work. He walked her to the office of Woods & Carter and thanked her for having lunch with him.

"Could we do this again sometime?" he asked as they stopped in front of the glass doors.

She hesitated and he thought perhaps she was going to refuse.

"Yes. I'd like that."

She was looking at him with those pools of brown eyes and he realized that he really did want to see her again...and not only just to learn more about Woods & Carter.

Chapter 7

How long should he wait to call Katie? He didn't want to seem too anxious, didn't want to tip his hand with all the questioning. But there were still questions that needed answers. And, besides, he had genuinely enjoyed Katie's company. But Nash decided it was too soon.

The legal pad of paper on the top of his desk had doodles all over it. He tore the top sheet from the tablet; and forming it into a small ball, aimed it at the wastebasket. It fell short. No solutions seemed to be coming to him. A knock at the door interrupted his thoughts.

"Come in," he responded.

Again came the knock on the door.

"Come on in. The door is open," he raised his voice.

The door slowly opened and in walked the timid Anne carrying a foil package.

"Oh, hello, Anne," Nash said getting to his feet. "Come right on in. You don't have to knock."

"Hello," she answered, giving a shy look around the sparsely furnished room.

Then, as if she had indeed lost track of her reason for being there, she brought her focus back to him.

"Papa said you might be hungry."

She awkwardly thrust the package at him.

"Well, that wasn't necessary."

"Papa likes you," she said simply. "And you helped us the other day."

"I like him, too. He's a really thoughtful man. Your Papa is a good person."

She seemed happy for his comment about her father, but immediately became self- conscious again.

"I should go," she said.

"You can stay and talk with me for a while if you want."

"You're not busy?"

"Well, I have been working on a case, but I'm kinda stumped right now," he admitted.

"Being a private detective must be exciting," she seemed interested.

"Well, sometimes," he said, "but it's not always as glamorous as it might appear."

Attempting to change the subject, he studied the little face before him.

"How about you, Anne? What are you interested in?"

She visibly blushed and again was uncomfortable.

"Oh, my life is not very exciting. I go to school and help Mama and Papa in the delicatessen and do my homework."

"Where do you go to school?"

"Oh, I'm a junior at St. Anthony's high school."

"Yes, I know about St. Anthony's. As a matter of fact, my little brother's soccer team is playing St. Anthony's today after school. Will you be there?"

"Oh, no, I don't go to things like that. Papa expects me to be home to help with the store... and there's always homework."

"I see."

"Well, I gotta go. Papa will be wondering what happened to me."

"You come back anytime, Anne," he encouraged. "And thanks for the sandwich. Tell your Papa I appreciate his thoughtfulness."

She nodded and smiled and slipped out the door.

Nash hadn't realized how hungry he was. A glance at his watch reminded him it was two o'clock and he had indeed missed lunch. And he wanted to get to Tony's soccer game, thinking it was important to support his little brother. Little brother? Not for long. Tony was really in a growth spurt. He was already almost as tall as Nash and had put on quite a few pounds...mostly muscle...in the past year. Yes, Nash needed to spend as much time as he could with Tony before he was all grown up.

The stands were filling up by the time Nash reached the soccer field. That didn't take a whole lot. Soccer wasn't nearly as popular as football and the section for seating was rather small. Scanning the field, he found Tony and raised his hand and saw the response. Now Tony could comfortably concentrate on the game knowing Nash was there rooting for him.

But Nash was not the last fan to arrive. At first, he couldn't believe his eyes. Short brown hair and dark rimmed glasses were the first things to catch his attention. Work place clothes had been replaced with a pair of blue capris and a blue and yellow casual shirt. She carried a wide brimmed hat and a huge straw tote. All he could do was catch his breath. What were the chances? He scanned St Anthony's team and wondered which player was Katie's brother.

Trying to be discreet, he kept an eye out to see where she would sit. Apparently Katie was by herself. Nash tried desperately to concentrate on the game, all the while thinking about how he could approach her again without seeming too obvious or anxious.

But it was in the last quarter when Tony made a drive with the ball towards the goal and executed the left footed kick which sent the ball past the goalie for the score that did it. Nash was on his feet, yelling at the top of his lungs. Tony high fived several players on the field and then looked towards the stands to see his big brother on his feet, wildly flailing his arms. Tony waved an acknowledgement. So involved was Nash with the game that he failed to notice the petite girl who turned to see what kind of maniac was causing such an uproar. Could it be? Was this the same guy she'd had lunch with a few days earlier? She pulled the straw hat closer to her face and hoped he didn't notice how often she peeked his direction throughout the rest of the fourth quarter.

St. Anthony's was going down in defeat and the soccer field was one of celebration for Tony and his teammates. Gathering himself together to head towards Katie, Nash came up short. The space where Katie had been sitting was empty. Oh, no. He'd lost the chance to engage her in conversation. Not a meeting where he was intentionally searching for information. He was disgruntled to say the least. Oh, well, he hadn't really expected to see her at the soccer match anyway so it wasn't planned or anything, but he saw it as a lost opportunity. As those thoughts raced through his mind and as he pushed his way through the crowd toward the exit gates, he was surprised once again when he sensed someone walking close to his right arm. Looking down, he saw the dark rimmed glasses and nearly stopped right where he was.

"Where'd you come from?" he asked.

"Any law that says I can't attend my little brother's soccer game?" she replied.

"Free country," he smiled.

"But I'm not a very good loser," she was stern.

"Umm. My guess is your brother plays for St. Anthony's," he mumbled.

"As a matter of fact," she stated, "my brother is the goalie. I believe it was your brother who scored two goals against him."

"Ouch," Nash flinched. "Sorry 'bout that."

"Well, you're probably not too sorry since your team won the game."

He smiled a sinister smile.

"Guess you're right. We do like to win."

"I shouldn't say this, but your little brother is quite a talented player."

Nash stopped short.

"How do you know which player was my brother?"

"Oh, I don't know," she said sarcastically. "Perhaps it's because you were the one who was jumping around like a maniac when he scored a goal. Either he was your brother or you are just a complete idiot."

"Thanks for that."

Nash found himself smiling; and when he looked at Katie's face, he realized most of what she said was teasing him.

By this time, the crowd had thinned out and they were approaching the parking lot.

"By way of apology for my extreme antics, perhaps we can do lunch again sometime," he suggested. "Unless you're afraid to be seen in public with a possible idiot."

He smiled and she returned his smile.

"Sure. Why not? It's the least you can do since your team won."

"We could go to dinner right now, but I have to take Tony home."

"That works out okay. I am picking up my little brother as well."

At that point, Tony came running up.

"Did you see that, Nash?" he was excited. "Did you see me score?"

"I sure did," Nash said, giving Tony's head a congratulatory rub. "Great job!"

"The goalie just didn't have a chance, did he?"

Nash glanced at Katie.

"Uh, Tony, meet the other goalie's sister."

Tony's look of embarrassment was evident.

"I'm sorry," he apologized.

Katie laughed.

"No need. It was a good play. Congratulations. You're an outstanding player."

A broad grin spread across Tony's face.

"Thanks."

"We should go," Nash explained. "How about tomorrow?"

"Tomorrow is great," Katie smiled. "You know where to find me."

"Sure thing."

"You ready, Nash? I'm starved," Tony said as he wiped his face with a piece of old towel he carried for games.

Katie watched as Nash and Tony crossed the parking lot to the '85 Chevy with the dented door. She would look forward to tomorrow.

———————●◖●◗●———————

"Can you fix me up with a picnic lunch?" Nash asked Mr. Meijer.

"Ah, a special lunch?" Mr. Meijer gave him a knowing glance.

Nash smiled.

Mr. Meijer turned to his wife.

"Mama," he smiled, "I think our Nash is courting a young lady."

Nash appreciated their support.

"Actually," he said, "it's kinda sorta like working on a case."

"Ah, I see."

"Put extra dessert in, Mama. He needs to sweeten up someone."

They both smiled and Nash nodded in return. The Meijers were good people.

Katie seemed really pleased with the adventure of sharing lunch in the park. Once comfortably situated on a green painted bench under the shade of one of the majestic oak trees that lined the park path, Nash opened the contents of the lunch...the one that had been packed with care at Meijer's delicatessen. And Mr. Meijer was receiving many rave reviews from Katie on having outdone himself with the picnic lunch. Nash was pleased as well that she thought his idea of lunch in the park was a good one.

He noticed the spring colors in her dress which made her look a little less like a secretary and a lot more feminine in his opinion. There was a sense a freeness about her today.

"This is a wonderful idea," she began. "And you're really good at finding great food."

"Thanks. My office is right above a delicatessen and the Meijers are great folks. Actually, your little brother may know their daughter. Anne goes to St. Anthony's, too."

"Could be. I don't know the name. But the Meijers must be good people if they can prepare food like this," she complimented, taking another bite of Mrs. Meijer's famous potato salad.

"Yeah. You know, encouraging the small businessman, the backbone of America," he quoted.

She remembered the conversation from their first lunch at the neighborhood café.

"Are you making fun of me?" she challenged.

"Not at all," he replied, "just quoting someone's opinion I am learning to respect."

She seemed satisfied with his explanation and continued to crunch a dill pickle Mr. Meijer had tucked in the lunch bag. They watched as inquisitive squirrels scampered about, daring to come within a few feet of them, hoping for a tasty morsel to fall their way.

He waited what he considered to be a respectable length of time.

"Are things settling down now for you at the office?" he asked.

Putting her sandwich aside, she uttered a sigh.

"Some, I guess. As a matter of fact, the new Mrs. Woods was in the offices today. Maybe she came to pick up some personal items from Mr. Woods' desk. I really don't know why she was there."

He waited for more, interested in the way she referred to the two women as the first Mrs. Woods and the new Mrs. Woods, but more did not come.

"I'm guessing there's an opinion in there somewhere," he nudged.

"Umm, we all liked the first Mrs. Woods. She was kind and cheery and always took time to chat with people, no matter what position they held in the company. It's just been difficult to adjust to someone else. Although the new Mrs. Woods is a beautiful woman...and friendly enough. Gina's her name. Just not what we're used to, I guess. Just not the same. Today she spent a lot of time in Mr. Carter's office and I think she'd been crying when she came out."

Nash thought about that for a few moments. He chose to concentrate on Mr. Carter.

"Well, you indicated the other day that Mr. Carter may not be the most sympathetic person. Perhaps I didn't say that correctly. Maybe just not a people person."

She nodded, once again relishing the sandwich.

"Were they close...the Woods and the Carters?"

"I don't think so," she answered. "The men seemed to get along together okay, but I never saw much between the two women."

Katie thought again.

"However, I did overhear some raised voices between Mr. Woods and Mr. Carter a few weeks ago. I just happened to be delivering some correspondence to Mr. Carter's office and the two men were there. I knew they were having a disagreement, but I couldn't understand the words. I just turned around and went back to my desk. Shortly after that, Mr. Woods asked me to place a call to his attorney, which I did."

"Wow, lots of drama goes on in an office. I never realized."

"You're not hungry?" she asked, noticing he hadn't eaten much of his sandwich.

"Oh, yeah, not real hungry," he faltered. "Guess I'd rather talk with you."

Nash had probed as far as he thought would be wise and spent the rest of the time learning more about Katie, the woman. While she liked her job at Woods & Carter, she had ambitions of returning to college and perhaps earning a degree in business. She had put off having a relationship because she was concentrating on helping her mother and getting her little brother...the goalie for St. Anthony's soccer team...through high school. Nash and Katie had a lot in common.

———————•◉•———————

It was time to make contact again with the Woods' family.

"Hello."

"Hello, Gina, this is Nash...Nash Adams."

"I know," she purred. "So good to hear your voice, Nash."

Why was it that when he heard hers, his heart began to beat more rapidly?

"How are things going?" he delayed the purpose of his call.

"About like I imagined," she responded. "I think Candy is right when she says we're a dysfunctional family. I've tried, Nash. I've really tried with the children. But without Stephen here to be a buffer, so to speak, I just feel like I'm losing the battle."

Thinking she was on the verge of tears, he tried to divert the conversation a bit.

"Everyone deals with grief in a different way," he said. "Give it some time."

He heard the sniffles.

"And now the will is to be read tomorrow morning," she was audibly shaken. "And I really don't know what's in it. Stephen and I never discussed it and I don't know what to expect or how the children will react. I don't want another scene and more drama. Nash, will you come and be present at the reading of the will?"

Would he? There was nothing he'd like to do more. Perhaps there was something in Stephen Woods' will that would shed some light on this case.

"Sure, I could do that."

"Good," she told him. "Ten in the morning at the offices of Harrington and Hampton. Thank you so much, Nash. Maybe with you there, things will go smoothly."

———————•◉•———————

Smoothly wasn't exactly the word to describe the outcome of the reading of the will.

There's something cold and unfriendly about attorney's offices. Perhaps it's the imposing amount of books that line the walls. Could anyone ever know what information was in that many books? Nash compared the atmosphere of talking in hushed tones to those of being in a funeral home. A rather solemn looking woman with her gray hair piled high on her head and wearing a navy blue suit glided across the reception area to open a door for the family and Nash as they entered a room full of rich mahogany wood furniture and were greeted by a man wearing a steel gray suit from behind the most massive desk Nash had ever seen. It was smooth and shiny and there wasn't a scratch on it anywhere.

When they were all comfortably seated in leather chairs that reeked of money, Mr. Harrington took an envelope from his desk drawer; and holding it in his hand for all to see, announced that Stephen Woods' will had been revised a month or so ago under the auspices of the law offices of Harrington and Hampton.

Nash made a mental note as to why Stephen Woods had felt the need to revise his will so close to his own death. That could send this case in an entirely different direction.

Taking the document from its envelope, Attorney Harrington began to read:

I, Stephen Woods, being of sound mind...

It was at this point Candy Woods broke into a sob and Cliff moved to console his younger sister. Lindy crossed and re-crossed her long legs and Susan stared straight ahead, apparently with no emotion at all. However, Susan dug in her purse for a tissue and pushed it into her little sister's hand, almost with an unspoken demand to straighten up and stop sniveling.

Mr. Harrington scanned the group before him over his glasses which were perched on the end of his nose and then continued reading.

Nash cut through all the legal jargon and focused on the facts. Stephen Woods' will was a surprise to everyone. Cliff was to retain ownership of the house on Hickory Lane with the stipulation that Gina would live there as long as she wished. Lindy got the property on the southern coast, Candy had ownership to the property in the east and Susan was to have the hunting lodge. The household staff had been provided for, but the biggest surprise came when Mr.

Harrington read that all other monies and assets were to go to Tammy Woods.

Gasps could be heard all around the room.

Tammy? The first Mrs. Woods? The divorced Mrs. Woods? The mother of his four children? Needless to say, Tammy Woods would be a very wealthy woman.

Attorney Harrington waited for a few minutes to let the terms of the will sink into the minds of the recipients.

"Stephen Woods' final words in his will are:

'I know all of you are upset by my decisions. Please do not be. It is for your own good. You have been privileged children and it is time for you to figure out how to manage on your own. You are all smart and capable enough to build your own lives and fortunes. Good luck. I love you all.' "

Mr. Harrington laid the document on the desk and removed his glasses. Leaning back in his chair, he brought his fingertips together and appeared to be contemplating what he would say next.

"I am aware this is not at all what you expected to hear. But, I assure you that Stephen knew what he was doing. I will inform Mrs. Woods...the first Mrs. Woods...of the contents of the will. Are there any questions?"

"The hunting cabin?" this from Susan Woods. "There must be some mistake. Surely father could not have remotely thought I would be interested in that. And now that it has become the crime scene..." she faltered. "What are the procedures to contest the will?"

"That is not feasible at this point," Mr. Harrington attempted to explain.

Candy turned to Gina.

"How does it feel to be cut out of the money entirely, Gina?" she confronted. "You knew about this all along, didn't you? That's why you killed him. He wasn't going to leave anything to you."

Gina was clearly emotional at Candy's outburst.

"Lay off, Candy," Cliff defended. "Gina has a home on Hickory Lane for as long as she wishes."

"Oh, yeah, right, Cliff," Susan stood. "You just want to have Gina where you can have easy access. Are you and that that... woman... guilty of murdering our father?"

So far Susan had accused Gina, Lindy and Cliff of being involved with Stephen's murder. Was she attempting to deflect suspicion from herself? Nash wondered.

"Susan, we are all upset about Daddy's death. Just don't say something you'll regret later."

This from Lindy Woods. Perhaps there was more to this blonde jetsetter than there appeared to be. Could she turn out to be the most level headed one of the bunch?

Realizing there was no more to be said from Mr. Harrington, the group stood to disperse.

"Oh, I feel faint," Gina gasped, putting her hand to her forehead.

Cliff rushed to her side; and offering her support, helped her to a chair.

"Give her some air," he demanded.

"Oh, great, more drama," Susan spoke from an area far removed from the scene.

"Gina, you've got to be the best actress ever...pretending you care," Candy spit.

Cliff attempted to fan Gina while she indeed looked rather pale and kept her eyes closed.

Lindy appeared with a glass of water which she handed to Cliff; and he in turn, offered it to Gina.

Chapter 8

Following Candy Woods was a piece of cake. She was very visible in her blue sports car and campus was a busy place, a place to easily blend in. Plus being there brought back memories for Nash of being enrolled there in classes; but that seemed like another world, time before Pop had passed away. Bennington College was much like any other small college, easy to negotiate. It was finals week at the college and Nash observed Candy from afar as she made her way to class and then to the library. He chose the trip to the library as a good opportunity for observation. Being situated out of sight in the stacks of books and close enough to the table where Candy and her friends were sitting, Nash hoped he would be able to hear their conversation. Taking a book from the shelf and keeping his back to the table, he pretended to be searching through the book for a specific page.

Then, putting the book in front of his face, he looked beyond the corner of the shelf to see who the players were in this scene. There were two young men and two girls sitting with Candy at the table. One of the girls had bright red hair cut short in the back and long around her face, obviously not her own color, and wore what appeared to be orange lipstick. Putting that together with her pink top caused Nash to think she resembled a circus clown. The second girl had dark hair and wore lots of eye shadow. Interest in her face was overshadowed by the low cut top she wore which caused Nash to wonder if it hadn't been available in the next larger size.

The young man sitting next to her could hardly concentrate on anything other than the girl sitting next to him. A shock of blonde hair and an extremely tan body and bright blue eyes were accentuated by the shades of the blues in his shirt. The second boy, the one who was sitting next to Candy, wore rather thick glasses and had a nervous laugh to almost every comment that was being made.

Nash needed a picture; but wondered if, being this close, the sound of the camera would give him away. Aiming the lens towards the group, he coughed at about the same time he hit the button and surmised that no one seemed to have noticed. Good.

He discreetly turned around and pretended to be interested in the book once more. He was so engrossed in listening, he barely noticed a person from the library staff who was shelving books. Peering at him over her glasses and giving him a stern look, she maneuvered in front of him.

"Excuse me," she whispered.

"Oh, pardon me," Nash said as he apologized for being in her way and quickly moved to one side.

She scowled at him over her glasses as she continued looking for Dewey Decimal numbers.

Conversation from the table of college students floated to his ears.

"Oh, you poor thing! I can't imagine having to be humiliated like that, Candy."

Nash tried to match the comment with the person and concluded it must have been the colorful girl.

"It was awful!"

That voice he recognized. It belonged to Candy Woods.

"I'm here to tell you that I have put up with the wicked stepmother long enough. I'm moving out!"

"Does that mean we won't be going to the beach house next month?"

That was a male voice, but no giggling so that had to be the blonde guy with the tan.

"I hope not, Stan," Candy replied.

Okay, the blonde guy was Stan.

"We'll all need a break after school's out."

That was the second male, the one with the giggle in his voice.

"Brad, you're always on break whether school's in session or not," the colorful girl admonished.

"Hey, Sissy, I earn every grade I get," Brad retaliated.

"It's not hard to earn a D," Sissy continued.

Nash was forming mental images as they spoke. Sissy was the colorful girl, Brad was the one who giggled a lot, Stan was the blonde. What of the other girl at the table? Apparently she had not spoken.

"You have to go to summer school?" Stan asked.

"Only if I want to graduate on time," Brad answered. "I don't really think my parents care that much either way. My grades are no secret, no surprise to them."

"Candy, please know that we will keep your secret."

That was a new voice. This had to belong to the dark haired girl with the plunging neckline.

"Thanks, Clare, I knew I could count on you."

"I am so sorry this has happened to you. I had hoped there would be another alternative, but I understand how you came to this decision."

Clare was certainly empathetic to whatever Candy's problem was. There were several murmurs of agreement and understanding from among the group.

"Gotta go," Candy said as Nash heard a shuffling of chairs. "Can't be late for this exam. Professor Frost said he'd close the doors promptly at 11. What a dufus! See you later, guys."

Candy was gone and the others didn't linger.

"She can't keep this secret forever. Sooner or later somebody's gonna find out," Clare said.

Nash folded his notebook and put his pencil in his chest pocket. Turning, he nearly ran into the librarian who was still shelving books.

"Sorry, ma'am," he apologized for the second time.

Once again the librarian gave him an angry look as he made his way out of the book stacks and into the sunlight. So, Candy Woods was harboring a secret.

Lindy Woods left the house on Hickory Lane in her Mercedes; and although Nash intended to follow at a discreet distance, he wondered if his old Chevy was going to be able to keep up with the Mercedes as it darted in and out of traffic. However, he still had her in his sights when she wheeled the vehicle into a parking space at the marina. He slowed a bit and watched as the blonde beauty emerged from the car, put on her sunglasses, slung her bag over her shoulder and made her way towards the bar area of the marina.

Nash found a parking place on the far side of the parking lot under the shade of some nearby trees. The Chevy lacked air conditioning; and parking there might make it more comfortable for him when he came back to the car. Removing his sunglasses as he entered the door of the bar, he scanned the tables and booths until he spotted the blonde hair. She was seated across from a man whose black hair was slicked back against his head. Luckily her back was to Nash and a divider filled with tropical plants separating booths from the bar provided Nash the protection he needed. So Nash made his way to a booth directly opposite of the one Lindy and the man she was meeting occupied.

He had gotten a pretty good look at the man, not at all the kind of person one would expect to keep company with the gorgeous Lindy. He somehow expected a young tanned guy with a nautical look to be in her company. Instead, this man was older and dressed mostly in black and kept nervously looking over his shoulder. A scar down his left cheek, a small goatee and a rather large flashy ring on one hand were noted by the young investigator.

Nash wanted to part the greenery separating the two booths, but thought that unwise. He would have to settle for overhearing some conversation.

"Thank you," Lindy was saying.

"Satisfaction guaranteed," the man answered.

There was a slight accent, but Nash couldn't place it.

"Here's the amount we agreed on," Lindy whispered.

There was a pause.

The waitress chose this time to take Nash's order.

"What'll it be?" she asked.

"Just a regular coke," he said in low tones.

"That it?"

"Yes. That will be all."

The waitress left and Nash continued listening, hoping he hadn't missed anything important by the interruption.

"It's all there," Lindy said, "as we agreed."

"I always double check."

"I would never think of cheating you."

"I hope not."

Another pause.

"It's all here," he declared. "Call me if you ever need my services again. You know how to contact me."

Nash sensed the man was preparing to leave.

"Tell Guido I said hello when you see him."

If Lindy said anything more, he didn't hear it.

Nash could see the top of the man's head now that he stood up and Nash had to hurry to get ahead of him. Once outside, he positioned himself and readied his camera. Continuing to nervously scan the parking lot over his shoulder and overlooking the young investigator, the man made his way towards a black sedan and Nash took aim. Zooming in, the shutter clicked and Nash added another photo to his collection. Nash stayed long enough to see the lovely Lindy exit the building and make her way to a yacht docked at the marina. Nash wrote down The Night Queen in his notebook and headed for his car.

Inside the bar, a bewildered waitress stood with a regular coke in her hand and no customer.

Louie took the photo from Nash's hand and studied it carefully.

"Can't say that I recognize the face, although he does look familiar. Something about the way he's dressed. Sometimes you get a feel for things like this after a while. Let me make a copy of this. Something just might surface when you least expect it. What are you thinking?"

Nash was quick to share his thoughts.

"What do you think about possible mob connections? Hired gun? Hired thug? Something he was paid a sum of money for."

Louie studied the photo again as he walked from the copy machine.

"Could be," he mused. "Could very well be. You are welcome to look through the books anytime you want."

Nash had taken up enough of Louie's time; and noticing that the stack of file folders on the edge of Louie's desk had not diminished, he decided he should go.

"Thanks," he said, extending his hand.

Louie shook hands and clapped Nash on the back.

"Keep in touch," he encouraged. "Remember: good guys win, bad guys lose."

Nash had been down the street from the house on Hickory Lane since 6 a.m. Either Cliff Woods hadn't spent the night at the house or he was getting a late start to the day. Glancing at his watch, Nash realized it was 9 o'clock already. He reached for the cup of coffee which was now cold and rummaged in the white bag which held a fresh doughnut from the small doughnut shop not far from his office. Another small business. He smiled at that.

Another hour passed and Nash was just ready to call it a day and approach a different avenue when he saw the garage door open and watched as the jaguar roared out of its cage. Cliff must have been in a hurry or else it was his style to drive fast because he took off at a terrific rate of speed and Nash pushed his old Chevy to fall in at a comfortable and inconspicuous distance behind him.

Cliff seemed to be heading for the north side of town and Nash's brain was working overtime to try to remember what was on the north side of town that would interest Cliff Woods. And then it loomed in front of him...the new twelve-story hotel...The Gateway. Nash had heard about this place. Very expensive and exclusive. Complete with bar and restaurant and who knows what else, exclusive to the rich. After watching the taillights of the jaguar pull into the parking garage, Nash tripped the machine that dispensed the parking tickets and made his way up the ramp. Cliff passed up parking spaces on the first levels. At level nine, he slowed and appeared to prefer to park at this level. Nash pulled on past him and kept an eye in his rear view mirror. When he was sure Cliff had found a spot, Nash pulled into the last parking space on the end and watched as Cliff went into the elevator. The elevator light stopped on level eleven. If Cliff Woods' destination was indeed level eleven, why had he parked on level nine?

Starting the Chevy again, Nash checked out level eleven of the parking garage. Plenty of spaces there. Plenty of expensive cars as well. It looked like a lineup of the best of the best. Making his way back to level nine, Nash once again parked his car and took the elevator. Try as he might, every time he chose floor eleven, the elevator refused to make a stop there. After several attempts, Nash got off on floor ten and found the stairway. He was rapidly losing track of his suspect. Once again he found the door to floor eleven inaccessible.

Nash made his way to the first floor restaurant; and finding an empty stool at the bar, he slid into the seat. After checking around the room, he was convinced he did not recognize anyone.

The bartender swiped the bar with a wet towel and laid a napkin in front of him.

"What'll ya have?"

"Uh, oh, root beer, please."

Giving him a puzzled look, the bartender shuffled off and returned a few minutes later with the soft drink.

"Drinkin' heavy today, eh?" he inquired.

"Yeah, I'm just waiting for my boss. I'm driving so need to be sober."

"Believe it or not, that happens a lot," the bartender volunteered.

Nash saw an opportunity.

"Yeah, the boss is up on the eleventh."

Nash tossed it out and watched for a reaction.

"Oh, yeah. One of those."

Okay, one of those what? Nash wondered.

"Hope he's not too late tonight," Nash ventured. "I got plans for later."

"Guess that depends on whether he's winnin' or losin'," the bartender commented and then moved on to another customer.

Gambling? That's sure what it sounded like.

Nash thought of a plan; and removing his cell phone from his pocket and placing it to his ear, he pretended to have received a phone call. He made sure the bartender was close enough to hear his side of the conversation. When he put the phone back in his pocket, he turned to the bartender once more.

"Now I'm in a fix," he admitted. "Family emergency and I have no idea how to get in touch with my boss. You got any ideas?"

"You don't have a card?" the bartender asked.

"Nope. I just usually sit around and wait 'til he shows up."

"A fifty will get you on the floor, but you have to know somebody to get to the back room. But maybe there's somebody up there who can get a message to your boss."

"Where do I get the card?" Nash tried not to sound desperate while he mentally tried to figure out if he had fifty dollars in his wallet.

"The Hulk," he halfway whispered.

The bartender pointed to a rather stern looking, hefty bald headed man in a suit standing over to one side of the crowded room. Nash hoped he'd never meet this guy in a dark alley; but after hearing Nash's story and looking him over and accepting the fifty dollars, the Hulk decided Nash was okay.

"Follow me," he grunted.

And Nash followed the towering Hulk through a dark corridor to a private elevator. No conversation took place and Nash was somewhat relieved when the door opened and Hulk gave him a nod.

Nash stepped into a smoke-filled room of slot machines and gambling tables. Choosing a seat at a machine off to one side and out of the mainstream but where he had a good view of the room, he pretended to be using one of the machines. There were little old women and young girls and men dressed in fashionable clothes and some seedy looking characters, but he did not see Cliff Woods anywhere among them.

Floorwalkers, as he chose to call them, kept an eye overall. When Nash became acclimated to the room, he began to move around trying to avoid suspicion. After paying the fifty dollars to gain access to floor eleven, he barely had five dollars in his pocket. Having no interest in gambling and no money to indulge in the activity, he chose to pretend to be interested in the action at the gambling table; but all the time he was scanning the room in search of Cliff.

He had pretty much canvassed the entire area and thought perhaps it was time for him to leave, when there was some commotion coming from behind the doors at the end of the room. As his attention was focused on the sound, the steel doors opened and two men were pushing a third man through them. When the man being pushed regained his footing and stood up straightening his fashionable clothes, Nash recognized Cliff Woods. The man standing next to Nash chuckled.

"Pretty boy must have run out of money. Luck was no friend to him tonight."

Nash turned towards the man.

"Yeah," he uttered. "Guess so."

"Pretty Boy...he come here a lot?"

"Yep, he's a regular. But I hear he's in hock big time and that just ain't gonna float with these guys. You pay up or you pay."

When this man said the word pay, it had an ominous sound to it.

Nash almost felt sorry for Cliff. He could see that Cliff was clearly humiliated as he was being pushed towards the elevator. After waiting a respectable length of time and seeing the elevator arrive with more patrons, Nash decided it was safe for him to leave. The jaguar was missing from its space by the time Nash reached the ninth floor parking.

So Cliff Woods had a gambling problem.

Chapter 9

If Katie checked her calendar once, she checked it twenty times. It had been four days since the picnic in the park and she was beginning to wonder if Nash just never intended to call again. And furthermore, she was beginning to think she would really like for him to call.

"Psst!"

Katie looked around at the sound.

"Psst! It's me...Clarice...over here."

Katie found the short dark haired woman who normally occupied the cubicle a couple over from Katie's desk.

"Whatever are you doing, Clarice?" Katie whispered.

"Guess what I just heard," Clarice insisted.

"Now, Clarice, you know I'm not much for office gossip," Katie dismissed.

Clarice's eyes grew wide with her information.

"Oh, this isn't gossip. I saw and heard this with my own eyes and ears."

"Okay," Katie resigned. "What is it you've overheard this time?"

Rolling her eyes and maneuvering Katie into a more secure position, Clarice kept her voice low.

"Mr. Carter and the new Mrs. Woods," she stammered. "Right there in his office. I know I caught a glimpse of them in each other's arms. And then I heard him tell her that everything would work out. Their plan had been a great one and that no one would ever know if they both kept their mouths shut."

Katie sighed.

"Perhaps he was just consoling her."

"You don't just console someone with a kiss like that."

"A kiss? Really, Clarice, aren't you embellishing things just a bit?"

Clarice was indignant.

"I know kissing," she said, vehemently, "and this was a kiss."

Clarice rolled her eyes again for effect and nodded her head for emphasis.

"Well, I'm glad you told me," Katie said. "Have you told anyone else?"

Clarice moved her head from side to side.

"Then don't. Not just yet. Let me think about it before we decide to do anything."

Clarice started back to her cubicle and Katie walked to her own desk just as the glass doors opened and in came Nash.

"Hello," he said. "I was just in the neighborhood and thought I'd drop by."

"Glad you did," Katie tried to sound nonchalant, pretending she hadn't been thinking about him all morning.

"I don't have time for lunch today, but how about dinner?"

Katie frowned.

"Can't. This is the evening I spend some time with my grandmother."

"Grandmothers sometimes go to bed early. How about dessert after?"

Katie smiled. Yes, Grandmother Hale would indeed be in bed early. Katie hurriedly wrote an address on a scrap of paper and gave it to Nash.

"You can pick me up at this address about 7:30 if you like," she said.

Taking the paper from her hand and waving it in the air, he headed for the door with a wide grin on his face.

"See you at 7:30," he beamed.

Nash was almost relieved that Katie wasn't available for supper. Being around Ma's table served as a refresher for him at the end of the day; and besides, he'd missed too many family meals lately. It was Ma's boiled beef dinner...a cheap cut of beef, but it had been slow cooked all afternoon and Ma added potatoes and carrots to it when it was almost done. Home baked bread and fresh cabbage salad complimented the main course. And as a special surprise, there were fresh strawberries. A real treat.

If there was one thing Ma insisted on at mealtime, it was good table manners and good conversation. Problems had been brought to the table in times past and solved before dinner was over. Tears had been brought to the table in times past and been replaced with laughter. No one was judged. Everyone had a right to his or her opinion. All were encouraged in whatever situations were brought forward. The right course of action just seemed to become clear at Ma's table.

A good example of this was the time Midge needed to find a job; and after much discussion, a plan had come together that she should pursue a job in retail because Midge was a people person and she had a good eye for style and accessories. Hence, the job at the dress shop had emerged. Various school issues that were major for Tony when he came to the table found solutions.

"How's the case going, Nash?" Midge asked.

Nash placed a slab of butter on the warm bread in his hand.

"Not very fast," he answered. "I'm in the process of collecting information on all the major suspects, but so far nothing significant has emerged."

"It will," Ma encouraged. "Just be patient and use your powers of observation. You'll solve it. You always were good at seeing things others don't."

"Pass the potatoes," Tony requested.

"What did you say?" Ma was quick to chastise and teach.

"Please pass the potatoes, ma'am," he quickly corrected.

"Please," he added a second please in response to Ma's piercing eyes.

Taking the bowl and helping himself to a sizeable portion of potatoes, he continued to talk.

"You still seeing that girl?"

"I don't know if 'seeing her' is the right word. But, as a matter of fact, we're going to go for dessert tonight."

"Good," Tony was excited. "Guess if you're having dessert later, you won't need dessert here so I can have your share."

Nash fell silent. Ma watched her oldest son for a few minutes before she spoke.

"What's bothering you, son?" she inquired.

"I like the girl."

He paused.

"Her name's Katie."

Instead of asking more questions, Ma wisely waited.

"That's a nice name," she commented.

"Yes, she's a nice girl...and now I feel bad that I haven't been completely honest with her."

"Honesty is always the best policy."

"How have you been dishonest?" Midge asked.

"You may not want to know," Tony interjected.

Nash ignored his little brother's comment.

"It's just that I haven't told her I'm a private detective."

Ma waited and let him speak in his own time.

"Plus I've kinda used her to get some information," he confessed.

They continued to finish their meal for a few more moments of silence.

"Guess I know what I need to do," Nash said as he pushed his chair back from the table.

Ma smiled. She knew her children would make the right decisions.

Nash was surprised to find the address Katie had given him was not that far from his own neighborhood. As he stepped up on the small front porch, his foremost thought was to tell Katie the truth. Grandmother Hale was a delightful little lady and loudly whispered to Katie that she thought Nash was a handsome guy. Katie blushed and Nash smiled and gave grandma a hug which she readily accepted.

Once settled in the '85 Chevy, Nash felt his stomach tighten. He had to tell Katie the truth. And, although it was the right thing to do, he didn't look forward to her reaction.

"So this is your car," she began.

"Oh, yeah, at least my transportation," he responded, checking the traffic before he pulled into the intersection.

"Nice."

He glanced at her sitting beside him.

"You really think so?" he expressed his surprise.

"Oh, heck yeah," she said with enthusiasm. "It's a classic."

He laughed.

"Sometimes I question the difference between classic and a piece of junk."

"Well, I say it's a classic."

He noticed the set of her jaw and realized he might just as well agree with her and relieved she saw some value in the old Chevy.

They were at the soda shop and he still hadn't found what he thought was a good opportunity to bring up his confession. Well, he guessed it could wait a little longer.

It was a root beer float for her and he thought that sounded good as well.

"Two root beer floats," he ordered.

Floats in hand, they found a table in an out of the way spot and sat down to enjoy the treats.

"Your grandmother seems like a sweet person," he commented.

"I think so," Katie answered as she took a long draw of root beer through the straw and then moved the ice cream around in the glass.

"Grandparents are anchors...a big asset to the family."

Katie stopped eating and studied Nash's face.

"You really are a good person, Nash Adams."

That could be the best opening he would get all evening. He plunged ahead.

"Well, you may not think so once I tell you the truth about me."

Stopping abruptly, she looked at him with puzzled expression. Now where was this going?

"Katie, I've not been real truthful with you about who I am," he began.

A sinking feeling embraced her body.

"I told you I was in business for myself, and that's true. But what I didn't tell you is that I'm a private investigator...or personal investigator as I like to call myself."

The confused look on her face continued.

"When I first met you," he rushed on, "I was just trying to get information...and, well...well, you just kinda were at the right place at the right time."

"I still don't understand," she said, wiping her face with the napkin. "What possible information could I have to interest you?"

"The case I'm working on...well, it's the murder of Stephen Woods," he blurted.

Her eyes concentrated on the root beer float and Nash had a terrible feeling come over him.

"I see," she finally said softly.

An uncomfortable silence prevailed while both of them tried to process what was happening.

"Did you intentionally get to know me in the elevator that day?"

"Oh, no," he clarified. "You were just a girl I tried to help with her papers. It was after I realized that you worked for Woods & Carter that I used you. "

She thought a moment before she spoke.

"Would you have asked me to lunch anyway?"

"Probably."

"Then I see no harm done," she said and immediately began to focus again on the root beer float.

He sat staring at her, wondering if what he heard was true, relieved at her reaction to his news.

"So," she said, looking up at him once again, "have you found the murderer yet?"

"No," he answered. "Private investigating is not as glamorous as one might think. There's a lot of leg work involved."

"Umm."

Nash began to eat the ice cream part of the float.

"You may be interested in some office gossip," she offered. "Clarice...a girl in our office...told me just this morning that she had seen and overheard the new Mrs. Woods and Mr. Carter...in what was a rather compromising situation. But," she added, "you didn't hear it from me."

"You are amazing," he said. "I admitted I deceived you and still you are willing to help?"

"Umm," she said again as she gathered her purse as they prepared to leave. "I don't know as I'd go that far. Visions of you being a serial killer or a kidnapper are beginning to fade from my mind. And, besides, I would like to see Mr. Woods' killer brought to justice."

Nash smiled. Katie was okay.

After working with Louie down at the precinct to access some credit card records, Nash could have predicted where Gina Woods was going this afternoon. A call from Katie on his cell phone confirmed his beliefs...Mr. Carter would be out of the office this afternoon. Nash arrived at the Blue Star Motel before Greg Carter arrived. Gina's car was parked under a shade tree and Greg Carter's BMW parked at the opposite end of the parking lot. But Nash had clear photos of Gina and Mr. Carter as she opened the door to unit # 4. Nash waited for an hour and a half when he saw Mr. Carter exit room #4 and then Gina left a few minutes afterwards. Although he felt as if he had the information he needed about Gina Woods and Greg Carter, he continued to follow her throughout the afternoon as she made stops at the bank, the beauty parlor and an attorney's office. Now that piqued Nash's interest! He overlooked the black SUV that kept a safe distance behind him.

Susan Woods was a creature of habit. Therefore, it was easy to predict some of her movements. Every evening she stayed in the seclusion of her apartment with no apparent guests. Every day at precisely 1 o'clock, she appeared at the Easy Skillet for lunch. Sometimes she dined with business associates or friends or sometimes alone, but it was always the same table and the same waiter. The meals were usually solemn events, not filled with the good natured laughter and conversation often associated with restaurant meals. Nash had been observing the routine for several days without any suspicious activity. He had, however, a nice collection of photos of those who ate lunch across the table from Susan Woods.

Today would be no different. If nothing significant turned up, Nash would put his efforts elsewhere.

Nash had just ordered a bowl of soup when he sensed someone near him.

"Good afternoon, Mr. Nash," the voice was very businesslike.

He looked up into Susan Woods' stern face; and pushing back his chair, he stumbled to his feet.

"Oh, hello," he said, wiping his chin with the napkin. "You surprised me. I wasn't expecting to see anyone I knew."

Susan smiled as if she knew he was not being truthful.

"Really," she smirked. "You eat here often?"

"No, not often. I was to meet a client here, but I think he must have been detained."

"I see."

He stifled the feeling of trying to explain more about his presence at the swanky restaurant.

"Good to see you, Susan," he recovered.

"Good to see you, Mr. Nash," she replied.

With that remark she continued to her usual table and Nash continued with his soup. Evidently no one was meeting Susan Woods for lunch today. Nash was relieved when he felt comfortable enough to leave. As he turned, he nearly ran into Greg Carter.

"Oh, excuse me," he apologized.

"Yeah, watch where you're going," Greg answered gruffly.

"Hey, you're Greg Carter of Woods & Carter, aren't you?"

Greg looked cautiously around him before he answered.

"Why, yes," he said softly. "Have we met before?"

Mr. Carter clearly did not remember.

"Nash...Nash Adams," Nash said as he extended his hand towards Mr. Carter.

Ignoring his hand, Greg continued to frown.

"We met at your partner's funeral...Stephen Woods," Nash attempted to explain.

"Oh, oh, yes, Nash Adams, private investigator."

"Personal investigator," Nash corrected.

"Good to see you again, Adams," Greg said as he made his way towards the dining room.

Nash delayed long enough to see where Greg Carter was going. He slid into a seat opposite Susan Woods. Stepping behind a potted plant, Nash discreetly snapped another photo.

The '85 Chevy wove in and out of traffic along interstate 94 as Nash sped along the highway to the Detroit suburb. Music from the radio blared until he tired of it and turned the dial to the off position. He needed some peace and quiet. Facts from the Woods' case continued to swirl inside his head. Was his intuition failing him? He just couldn't get a handle on things. All were suspect and yet none of them had the motive Nash felt was strong enough for murder. Oh, yes, they had their differences and they all could be subject to suspicion, but murder?

Perhaps this trip to visit Tammy Woods...the first Mrs. Woods...would reveal something he could see as concrete.

The subdivision turned out to be exclusive; but Tammy Woods' house, although nice, appeared to be very modest, at least in comparison to the structure on Hickory Lane. Flowering shrubs were tucked in around the bungalow style house with its inviting winding brick walk that lead from the driveway to the front doors. The two car garage doors were open to reveal a Jeep Grand Cherokee. No butler came to let him in; no elaborate entrance. Instead, Tammy Woods opened her own front door. She was dressed in pink shorts with a multi colored blouse, looking fresh and cool on what was a rather warm day.

She was just as beautiful as he had recalled. Her dark hair was pulled back in a ponytail and she looked no older than any of her three daughters. And those gray eyes were huge and round and welcoming.

"Yes?" she questioned.

"Nash...Nash Adams? You remember, from the funeral...we met in the flower garden at the house on Hickory Lane?"

"Oh, oh, yes, Mr. Adams. Won't you come in? I didn't recognize you at first."

She opened the storm door and he walked past her into a small foyer and was immediately entranced by the delicious aroma coming from the kitchen.

"Am I intruding?" he asked. "I could come back later."

"Nonsense," she replied. "You are welcome here."

He nodded and somehow knew he would be.

After locking the door once again, she passed him and smiled.

"This way," she said softly and he followed her through the hallway, passing first a sitting room and then a cozy den where she stopped, inviting him in to see the array of family photos displayed on the fireplace mantle, photos that included pictures of Tammy and Stephen together. They appeared to be a typical happy family and Nash listened attentively as she told stories of the children's childhood. Yes, it appeared the Woods family had a happy life.

Overstuffed furniture clad in a plaid fabric in this room was of the comfortable variety. A large television screen was in one end of the room and Nash noted an assortment of guns in a gun cabinet on the opposite wall.

After leaving the den, they continued through sliding glass doors which opened onto a very small but well decorated patio with stone floor and a colorful assortment of potted plants. Beyond that, he saw sun glistening on blue water in a small swimming pool.

Large inviting chairs filled with pillows sat in the seclusion of tropical plants beside the pool and she gestured towards one of them. A pitcher of pink lemonade and a platter of cookies were waiting on a small table situated between the two chairs. Picking up a glass from the tray, she began to fill it with the tart drink.

"You seem like a cookie and lemonade kind of guy to me," she cooed.

He smiled, feeling totally comfortable in her presence, thinking she probably was tuned in to any guest who appeared on her doorstep.

"I thought I was the one who was to be a good judge of character," he smiled.

"I imagine you are," she said as she continued to pour from the pitcher and the tinkling of the ice as it hit the glass almost deafened him. Surely all his senses were heightened.

Filling a glass for herself, she sat down in the opposite chair; and crossing one slim tanned leg over the other, she smiled at him.

"Now what can I do for you?"

Nash moved in the chair and took a long sip of the lemonade.

"Just gathering more information. If there is anything at all that you can tell me..."

"Ask me anything," she offered. "I need to put this to rest as well, you understand."

Tears forming in her large gray eyes did not go unnoticed.

"You've heard from the attorney's office by now," he began.

Tammy sighed and put her hand to her forehead.

"Yes," she paused. "It was a shock. First Stephen's death and then the terms of the will."

She gave him a questioning look.

"You know the terms..."

"Yes," he nodded. "I am privy to that information."

"First of all," she continued, "those were in no way the terms of the will Stephen and I had made. Not that they had to be. After the divorce, he was free to change all of that, of course. Well, I guess that's what he certainly did. I had wanted him to patch things up with the children and now this has just seemed to make things worse. I want them to remember the man he used to be."

"Have you heard from the children?"

"Oh, yes. Of course Susan was the first to call. Madder than mad. I've been concerned about her. You know, when Stephen and I divorced, she was engaged to be married. But she called it off and has been anti men ever since. She has a real problem and I haven't been able to help her. I understand my children were children of privilege, but I wish he'd talked this over with me. I don't think the terms of the will accomplished what Stephen wanted. I think it was his attempt to make them responsible people. Instead, it has just brought more discontent."

"I hesitate to ask this," Nash continued. "Can you think of any reason why any of your children would commit an act of murder?"

She took the question as it was presented.

"Nash," she continued, "they all have had their difficulties. Susan has buried herself in her work and shoulders a lot of resentment. Lindy, well, Lindy is pretty much a free spirit. I don't know many of her friends and it's been suggested some of them could be connected with the mafia, but I'm not sure about that."

Nash's mind went to the man he'd witnessed talking to Lindy at the marina restaurant.

Tammy continued.

"And, yes, it's true that Stephen and Lindy often talked about her extravagant spending. Cliff is a climber. I know he's my son, but I also know he was disappointed that Stephen didn't take him into the company. And Candy? Well, she's still trying desperately to grow up and be her own person. She has a lot of deep feelings and is quite impressionable...and sometimes makes bad choices."

"Do you know of anything Candy could be hiding...like a secret that no one else...family...would know about?"

"No, not at all. Usually what Candy thinks comes out her mouth, a quality that sometimes gets her into trouble."

Nash thought about that for a moment. Did Tammy know about Cliff's gambling?

79

"In spite of the fact the children are well off financially, do any of them have any financial difficulties?"

Tammy seemed surprised at that question.

"I can't think of any reason," she answered. "Just what are you suggesting?"

"Oh, nothing specific. Just wondered if any of them could have invested unwisely or something like that."

"I would doubt that," Tammy relaxed. "Until now, Stephen would never have let them go under, so to speak."

Nash listened to the cubes of ice bump against each other as he drained the glass of lemonade.

"Good lemonade," he complimented.

"Here," she offered, "Let me fill your glass."

Taking the glass from his hand, she once again filled it and offered the cookies which Nash took time to enjoy.

"Homemade, aren't they?"

She smiled.

"Yes, they are."

Tammy Woods was a good cook as well. He was thinking that Stephen Woods had screwed up leaving Tammy. But then there was Gina.

"What's Gina's story?" he asked.

"Oh, Gina's okay. And Stephen is... was...a very attractive man. In my opinion, it wasn't the best choice he's made; but then, I don't know all the details. He probably did the right thing concerning her in the will. She is young and attractive and quite likely will move on."

Although Tammy spoke calmly and rationally about the subject, Nash sensed a unique quality in her voice when she spoke about Stephen and detected no hostility when she talked about Gina.

"What can you tell me about the relationship between Stephen and Greg Carter?" he prompted.

"Well, Stephen and Greg have been friends since college days. And they've been a division of the Nelson Corporation now for more than fifteen years."

"And Greg's wife?"

"Zoe? She and I were social friends. It was necessary for Stephen's position. I certainly hope I'm not talking out of turn here, but I don't think Zoe and Greg were happily married. She didn't go to college with us so I didn't know her well. It was like all of a sudden after Stephen and I married, Greg married Zoe. I don't know anything for sure, but I do know she has a drinking problem and I believe he has contributed to it."

"How so?"

"Greg likes women," she said bluntly.

"Did he ever approach you?"

It was out of his mouth before he thought about the consequences, but Tammy didn't flinch.

"Yes," she said firmly. "We dated some in college; but after Stephen and I were married, I gave him to understand I wasn't remotely interested and he never approached me again. He's a jerk. But he was Stephen's business partner and friend. And I do feel sorry for Zoe in a way. I don't think she would ever confront him about his problem so she just tries to deal with hers...by drinking."

Tammy glanced at her watch.

"I've stayed too long," Nash gathered his time was up.

"Oh, no, please stay," she begged. "Raoul is to come for dinner and I'd like for you to stay as well. I know how it is to be in a strange town and eating alone. This will be better than some restaurant. I guarantee. Come, we can continue our conversation in the kitchen while I finish up a few things."

"I can cook," she added as further incentive.

"In that case, I'd be willing to give it a try," he teased.

Tammy Woods' kitchen was comfortable. And she was comfortable in it. As much money as she had at her fingertips, she probably would always be at home in her kitchen, preparing her own meals.

"I could smell the roast cooking when I came in the door," he began as he inhaled the delicious aroma when she opened the oven door.

"I knew you were a meat and potatoes guy," she turned and her wide gray eyes smiled at him.

He smiled in return.

"What can I do to help?" he asked.

Before long he was tearing lettuce and dicing tomatoes and cucumbers and adding bean sprouts and other delicacies to a salad bowl.

Tammy set a beautiful table as if it was an everyday occurrence and had just lit the candles when Raoul appeared at the door. At first

Nash thought he felt a little resentment from Raoul at Nash's presence.

Nash extended his hand and offered some small talk and the tension appeared to have relaxed. He learned that Raoul had never been married and had no children. He liked fast cars and hanging out at the race track. And Raoul was very guarded about what he was willing to divulge.

Once seated at the table, Nash relished in the wonderful home cooked meal and felt as if he needed to restrain himself from looking like the struggling starving PI. But when the peach cobbler floating in cream and topped with a sprinkle of cinnamon was placed before him, he completely lost most of his good manners and restraint.

Although Raoul made his way to the den after the meal, Nash continued to help Tammy clear the table.

"We'll just let these dishes take care of themselves," she said as she placed them in a dishwasher. "We'll join Raoul in the den and see what he's up to."

See what he's up to? The statement struck him as odd, almost as if Tammy didn't trust Raoul to be alone in her house. But following her down the hallway to the den, he quickly forgot the remark. Raoul had made himself comfortable in one of the overstuffed chairs and had lit a cigar and was watching the evening news on television.

Tammy coughed and moved to open a window. It seemed that although Raoul was aware of her dislike for the smell, he intended to continue the cigar just for spite.

Situating himself in one of the oversized chairs opposite Raoul, Nash attempted to engage Raoul in conversation.

"Raoul, have you lived in this area all your life?"

Raoul took time to blow smoke at the ceiling as Nash waited uncomfortably for an answer.

"Between here and Chi town," he finally answered, not bothering to look away from the television to answer.

"Chicago? Really? Now there's a fascinating city."

Apparently that remark didn't require a response.

"Where did you meet Tammy?"

Raoul appeared to be annoyed with the questioning.

"Sorry," Nash apologized. "It's my job, you know…asking questions."

"Yeah."

"We met at one of Greg Carter's famous boring parties," Tammy filled in the information.

"And Tammy hasn't been able to keep her hands off me ever since," Raoul bragged.

Wishful thinking or was that sarcasm?

Tammy clearly was embarrassed by his remark. And remembering the conversation he'd heard in the gardens on Hickory Lane, he didn't think Raoul's comment seemed to fit their relationship.

Attempting to ignore his brashness, Nash forged ahead.

"Nice collection of guns," Nash said gesturing towards the gun cabinet. "Yours?"

Once again, not taking his eyes from the television set, Raoul answered.

"Mine. I like to feel protected."

"Actually, a couple of them are mine," Tammy added. "Stephen insisted on taking me hunting up at the cabin in the early years. He wanted me to know how to handle a gun."

Then with the realization that the cabin had been the site of the murder, Tammy was on the brink of tears once again. Nash thought he saw Raoul's body tense at the mention of Stephen's name.

Silence prevailed.

"What kind of business are you in, Raoul?" Nash tried to sound friendly.

"Export and import," came the short answer.

"Sounds fascinating," he responded.

"Can be. You meet all kinds in the business," Raoul replied as he continued to watch the evening news.

But Nash had picked up on the expensive suit and tie and the gold watch Raoul wore on his wrist. The import-export business must be very lucrative.

"Your own company?"

"Yes."

"Do you do business with Greg Carter? Or did you do business with Stephen Woods?"

Raoul turned towards Nash for the first time since the conversation started.

"You keep askin' questions, you might get some answers you won't like."

The anger in Raoul's eyes was unmistakable.

With that, Raoul stood and smashed the end of his cigar against the ashtray; and without a word, left the room. Apparently this interview was over. Nash heard the front door close behind Raoul without even so much as a good-bye.

Nash turned towards Tammy as if she had the answers he needed. He saw an intense hurt in Tammy's gray eyes.

"Raoul's not much on conversation...unless it's business," she attempted to explain.

"I got that impression."

Tammy seemed restless. And Nash knew unhappy when he saw it.

Nash found an excuse to leave. The dewy look in Tammy's eyes had disappeared. There was something amiss here. Was Tammy afraid of Raoul? He certainly didn't appear to treat her like the love of his life. As Nash started for the door, he turned one last time.

"Tammy, you don't have to stay with anyone who is unworthy of your company," he said simply.

She placed her hand on Nash's arm.

"Thanks. You're a good man, Nash," she said simply. "Find whoever killed my husband, please."

Choosing to stay in the Detroit suburbs another day seemed like a good idea. Following Tammy Woods didn't reveal anything, but watching Raoul's activities only added to Nash's distrust...especially when he saw Raoul escort a young woman into his lavish apartment. Also of interest was the other company Raoul kept. By Nash's best identification, these were foreigners...men in three piece suits and dark sunglasses accompanied by men Nash recognized as being body guards. Perhaps the import-export business was a dangerous business. He couldn't be positive, but one of the men suspiciously looked like the one Lindy Woods met at the marina restaurant. It was time Nash headed back home, his camera concealing more photos to add to his growing collection.

Chapter 10

Once back at the office, Nash spread the photos he'd taken out on the top of the desk. Each one told a story and yet there was a story hidden in each one as well. The yellow pad of paper was open before him and he absently twirled a pencil in his hand. His thoughts were interrupted by a knock on the door.

"It's open," he said while his mind was still on the photos before him.

The door opened slowly and Anne Meijer entered quietly, not willing to disturb Nash, softly closing the door behind her and stood shyly next to it. Nash looked up from his work.

"Oh, hello, Anne," he said. "I didn't realize you'd come in. You're so quiet."

She smiled shyly.

"You're busy," she said. "I'll come back another time."

"No, no. Come right on in. What's on your mind today?"

"Well," she began, making slight movements towards the desk, "I have a summer assignment to write a paper for one of my classes. And the teacher says we need to observe someone and write about their occupation. It's called shadowing. And, well….I…"

"And you thought you might want to write about being a private investigator?"

She nodded but immediately felt the need to apologize.

"Oh, I understand if you're too busy. I can always find someone else."

"Nonsense," Nash put her mind at ease. "I think it sounds like a great idea. But, remember, I told you my job is not as glamorous as people might think. You can start by putting down that this job requires a lot of thought process."

He gestured towards the notebook she carried and immediately she opened it and scribbled something down.

"For instance, on this case I'm working on…I've taken a lot of photos of people in different situations. One of them could end up being a suspect, but right now, they're just a bunch of photos without order or meaning."

Anne came over to the desk and scanned the photos.

"Maybe we should organize them on the wall so you can see them all from your desk. Then perhaps the meaning will come."

Nash smiled.

"That's a good idea, Anne. I think there's some tape here somewhere in this desk."

Having come up with the tape, Anne proceeded to organize.

"Is there a picture of the deceased?" she asked.

Nash furnished her with the photo Candy had given him of her parents and underneath their picture, Anne spread out the photos of each child in order of their age. Then she added out to the side of Stephen's picture, the photo of his second wife, Gina. At that point, she stood back to survey her work.

"These are beautiful women," she commented, her eyes wide with admiration.

"Yes," Nash agreed. "And one of them could be a murderer. Unfortunately, there is no clear description of what a murderer looks like."

"Who is this?" Anne asked as she picked up the picture of Raoul.

"That's the boyfriend of the first Mrs. Woods," Nash explained.

Anne placed Raoul's photo next to Tammy Woods.

"And this one?"

"The deceased's business partner, Greg Carter."

Anne put that photo off to the side and up to the right of Stephen's picture.

"Oh, my," Anne said as Nash handed her the next picture. "Isn't this the second Mrs. Woods with Mr. Carter? And aren't they outside a...a...a motel room?"

With that she clearly blushed with embarrassment. Then she moved Mr. Carter's photo and placed it next to Gina Woods. And her eyes widened at the photo of Mr. Carter in the company of Susan Woods. Shock crossed her face in reaction to the photos of Candy's college friends. Their world was far removed from anything Anne Meijer knew. The final photo was the one of the man who met with Lindy with The Night Queen looming in the background.

After spending a few minutes staring at the array of photos and discussing the circumstances that surrounded them, Anne spoke again.

"Maybe we should make a list of questions to pursue," she suggested.

"Good idea," Nash agreed, smiling at Anne's eagerness to participate.

Between the two of them, they came up with a list of questions to be explored. Nash was impressed with how Anne was able to organize and process detail. How far in debt was Cliff with his gambling and did he owe money to organized crime? Who owned the yacht Lindy was seen boarding and what kind of business transaction had been made with the man she met in the marina bar? Was the connection between Susan and Greg Carter one of business or pleasure? What was the secret Candy was keeping? Why did Gina Woods find it necessary to consult a lawyer? Did Zoe Carter know of her husband's indiscretion with Gina Woods? Did she care? Were Raoul's business connections in any way connected to his personal life?

Although it was getting to be late in the day, Nash decided to start his search by visiting the marina. Evening shadows were spreading their fingers across the parking lot by the time the old Chevy rattled into a parking place. Showing the photo of the man Lindy met with to the bartender in the marina bar revealed nothing. Although he'd seen Lindy in the bar several times, he did not recall having seen the man in the photo. No surprise there. Lindy was pretty noticeable. Going back into the night air, Nash spotted The Night Queen right away, gently rocking back and forth in her slip at the marina. It would be hard to miss the biggest, most auspicious yacht in the harbor. However, it appeared to be deserted. Water lapping against the dock made slapping noises before it swirled, seemingly trapped in the narrow space. Nash walked out onto the pier attempting to get a better look through the windows of the craft.

"Here now," a voice yelled from behind him. "You can't just go boardin' her without permission."

Nash turned abruptly, knowing that had exactly been his plan.

"She's a beauty, isn't she?" he said in a friendly manner. "I was just admiring her."

That seemed to calm the dock security worker some.

"That she is," he agreed. "None finer. You know yachts?"

"Not really," Nash continued. "I have a friend who has been looking into purchasing one and I've gone with him a few times to look. You wouldn't happen to know if this one is for sale, would you?"

The man shook his head.

"Doubt it."

Nash uttered an Umm as the two men continued to admire the boat in a moment of silence.

"You don't know who owns her, do you?" Nash ventured. "You're obviously a man who spends some time here at the marina."

"That I do. Keep an eye on things. Sometimes I take a few people out fishin' fer a few hours; but other than that, I'm pretty much around here most of the time just watchin' out fer these beauties."

With that, he gestured towards the array of well-kept yachts in their slips.

"And I know a lot of the owners of these jewels."

Nash waited.

"You know who owns this one?"

"All I know is they all wear either suits or fancy sailin' outfits and dark sunglasses. They ooze money, if ya know what I mean. And oh, yeah, and some of the most beautiful young women you've ever seen in your life come aboard her."

"I sure would like to get some more information. I think this is just what my friend might be looking for. If the offer is right, the owner might just be interested. You got any ideas as to how I could go about doing that?"

"Tell ya what...come back tomorrow about this same time and I'll see what I can find out."

"Thanks. I appreciate it," Nash said as he shook hands with the man and started back to his car.

"Who should I ask for?" Nash questioned.

"Name's Robert James Todd."

"Thanks, Robert James Todd."

Robert James Todd looked at the photo of the man who'd met with Lindy, but he had not recalled seeing him.

The sun was sinking fast and the parking lot already had shadows creeping across it. Nash reached the car to find a note taped to the steering wheel. He ripped it off and read the words: People who ask too many questions might not like the answers.

Nash turned his head to survey the parking lot to see if anyone was close by. That was the last thing he remembered before the lights went out.

When he regained consciousness, the moon was slipping behind a swirling sky. His vision reeled with the motion of the clouds. As his head began to clear, he struggled to his feet. Every muscle ached and his head throbbed; and when he put his hand to his face, it returned covered in blood. A split lip spewed blood and a knot was beginning to form on his head. Staggering and steadying himself against the side of the car, he reached for his billfold and that was still in his hip pocket and he felt his gun still in its holster. Nash looked around at a mostly deserted parking lot. Whoever had issued the warning was long gone.

Ma's concern was evident, but she demonstrated strength while she treated and bandaged his cuts and scrapes and did an excellent job of concealing the tears that flooded her eyes. Midge was quiet, listening carefully to the retelling of the incident. Tony, in typical teenage fashion, immediately thought they should find the guy and give him some of his own medicine. All in all, everyone in the family gave the exact responses Nash expected.

It had been a busy morning at Woods and Carter and Katie was elbow deep in papers. She was startled by the interruption.

"What happened to you?" Katie gasped as she looked up to see the doors to the office open and Nash walk through them.

"Don't know for sure. I think it was a warning."

He winced in pain as his face attempted a smile. Katie left her desk and escorted him to a more secluded section of the office.

"Who did this?" she demanded just as if she could do something if she had that information.

"I don't know. I was at the marina last night; and when I got back to the car, there was a note on my steering wheel and I turned to see who'd left it and the next thing I knew, I found myself on the ground."

Katie reached up to carefully touch his face.

"I'm so sorry," she sympathized.

Then her eyes grew wide as she came to a realization.

"But you know what this means, don't you?"

"Yeah," Nash said, shaking his head. "I need to be more careful when I'm reading notes left on my steering wheel."

He tried to laugh at his own humor and once again ended up in pain.

"Alright, wise guy," she cajoled. "But doesn't this mean you're getting closer to an answer in your case and someone doesn't want you poking around anymore?"

"Yeah, I get that. But who?"

Anne was clearly distraught to see Nash's face bruised and bandaged.

"Put down in your notebook that being a personal investigator comes with a few bumps and bruises," he attempted to be humorous.

The last thing he wanted to do was to alarm this innocent girl.

"Oh, I'm so sorry," she said, her eyes filling with genuine tears of compassion. "Did they take anything?"

"No," he said. "I checked. Everything was intact...even my gun. I believe it was purely to scare me. Someone is becoming a bit nervous about my questioning."

"Did you find anything out at the marina?"

"A little. I am to go back tonight and meet someone who might be able to shed some light on things."

"Be careful," the shy little girl admonished. "Should you take someone with you?"

"I'll be fine," he reassured as he put his arm around her shoulder. "Don't worry."

Anne nodded.

"I know you'll be fine, but you can't keep me from worrying."

Nash really had a lot of people who cared about him; and at this moment, he felt their support.

And Nash was super vigilant as he once again approached the waterfront. He wondered if Robert James Todd, the man he'd met last night, would even show up much less have any encouraging information. But he didn't have long to wait. He'd only been studying The Night Queen and her gentle sway in the water for a few minutes before he saw the figure heading towards him.

"Take a good look at her while you can," the man said. "She's set to sail later on this evening."

Looking at his watch, he added, "at about nine."

Nash took time to absorb that information.

"No luck?" Nash asked when the man seemed a bit reluctant to continue.

"Yes, I have some information for you."

With that the man pulled out a scrap of paper.

"The owner is a man by the name of Raoul Hoffer," he said, giving the paper to Nash.

Taking the scrap of paper in his hand, Nash had a sinking sensation in his stomach. Raoul? Raoul somehow connected to Lindy? Thanking the man for his help, Nash found a secluded table on the porch of the marina bar and waited. He wanted to know just who would be boarding The Night Queen this evening with Raoul.

Glow from the string of lights that danced in the evening breeze across the top edge of the porch did not reach the table where Nash sat waiting for 9 o'clock. He'd checked his watch at least five times in the past half hour. Sounds of clinking glass could be heard coming from inside the bar along with the notes of a country song wafting its way to Nash's ears. He was alone except for one couple at the far end of the porch who had no interest in the lone figure who sat waiting. Several times people had walked the pier, but no one had stopped near the yacht.

Then Nash heard the low tones of male voices talking followed by the sounds of girls giggling. Raising his glass to partially shield his face, Nash turned to watch as four people made their way down the pier and stopped in front of The Night Queen.

Only one of the four figures was recognizable. There seemed to be many facets to Raoul Hoffer's life.

Murder Among The Rich

Chapter 11

Bennington College was on summer break and Candy Woods was not enrolled in summer classes. As far as Nash could figure out, Candy's summer was being spent sleeping and sun bathing and hanging out with her friends until the wee hours of the morning. Nash could find nothing that revealed anything about any secret she may have been keeping.

Nash set up regular times to observe the Woods home; and after several of those sessions, he figured out that he was not the only one interested in the movements of the Woods' children. A black SUV hadn't been all that discreet and Nash concluded they were interested in Cliff Woods' activities rather than his and assumed their interest had something to do with Cliff's gambling debt.

The gun range over on the east side of town had become of great interest in the investigation. After making some casual inquiries and observations, Nash found out that the range was frequented not only by Susan Woods and Greg Carter, but also by Zoe Carter, Greg's wife. A gun in the hands of a neglected wife might be a hazard to someone's health.

Traffic was light on the return trip from the gun range and Nash's mind was busy with facts and questions about the Woods' murder but subconsciously his mind was fixed on the traffic pattern. A gray vehicle seemed to be taking the same path of traffic Nash was. Glancing in the rear view mirror, Nash realized the gray car was always there. A few unpredicted turns of the '85 Chevy revealed that the gray car continue shadowing his moves. Making a right turn down what he knew to be a dead-end alley, he screeched to a halt and ran to the gray vehicle that had blindly followed him into the trap. He had the driver's door open before the man had a chance to put his vehicle in reverse. Grabbing the driver by the collar, he pulled him from behind the wheel.

"Why are you following me?" he yelled as he pushed the startled man up against the side of the car.

"I...I...I wasn't following you," the man stammered.

"Sure you were. Tailing me in and out of traffic. I suppose you just accidently pulled into this alley way?"

Nash tightened his grip and pushed the man once more into the body of the car.

"Okay. Okay. Yes, I was following you. But...please...please don't hurt me."

"Why? Who are you?" Nash demanded.

"I was just hired to keep tabs on you, not to hurt you or nothin'."

"Who hired you?" Nash needed to know.

The man was visibly scared and not willing to withhold information when he felt threatened.

"Mr. Carter. That's who. Please, I was just doin' my job," the man pleaded.

"Why does Mr. Carter need to know what I do or where I go?"

"I don't know. He just asked me to watch what you did and report back to him. Honest. That's all I know."

Nash relaxed his hold on the man who he concluded was genuinely innocent in that he didn't know any more than he was being hired to tail Nash. He began to laugh.

"That's Greg, alright," Nash said. "He and I are always playing jokes on each other. And he got me good this time."

"Yeah?" the man laughed uneasily.

"What's your name anyway?" Nash asked.

"My name's Sam," the man appeared somewhat relieved.

Nash put his arm around Sam's shoulder.

"Well, you know, Sam, I'd sure like to continue this joke. How'd you like to help me? Oh, it doesn't involve anything terrible. Just something Greg and I have going between us."

Sam nodded and a slight smile began to cover his face.

"I've got a plan," Nash proposed, "and I need your help to pull it off."

Nash sensed Sam was on board with the scheme.

"I need you to tell Greg that you saw me going into the Blue Star Motel with this gorgeous woman. You got that? The Blue Star Motel," he repeated.

From there, Nash gave a detailed description of Gina Woods, one he was positive Greg Carter could easily identify.

Sam was nodding and smiling and seemingly pleased to be a part of such a good-natured joking between friends.

"Now you know, Sam, this will only work if you tell Greg like you were the one who saw the whole thing, don't you."

Sam nodded in agreement; and slapping Sam on the shoulder, Greg thanked Sam for his participation and they parted. Nash certainly hoped his plan might flush out more information.

————————•◆•————————

Nash's cell phone went off the following day about noon.

"Hello, Louie," Nash answered. "What's up?"

"I think I have a development in that case you've been working on. The Stephen Woods' murder?"

"Oh, yeah?" Nash questioned.

"Yeah," Louie answered. "Why don't you come on down to the precinct and we'll talk."

Nash paused, wondering what information Louie had that he didn't want to share over the phone.

As Nash pulled into the police station parking lot, a strange uneasiness overtook him. Taking the steps two at a time, Nash quickly arrived at Louie's crowded workspace.

"I came as soon as I could," Nash said. "You sounded pretty serious on the phone."

"Yeah," Louie replied.

Without divulging any more information and shoving some papers into a file folder, Louie got up from his desk and called to a fellow officer at the next desk.

"I'll be downstairs at the morgue," he announced and Nash went cold.

They walked in silence, boarded the elevator in silence and entered the morgue in silence. Louie talked to the person in charge in some low tones with words Nash could not understand.

"This way," the man said and they followed him into the coolness of the section where bodies were kept. Only then did Louie speak.

"I think this is the woman from your case," he said simply. "You want to identify her?"

The knot in Nash's throat prohibited him from speaking so he just nodded. Louie nodded to the man who in turn rolled the body out on the slab and carefully turned down the sheet that covered her face. Nash took one look and turned away. Louie put his hand on Nash's shoulder.

"You know her?" he whispered, half question, half statement.

Nash nodded.

"Yes. That's Gina Woods."

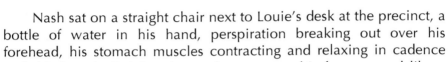

Nash sat on a straight chair next to Louie's desk at the precinct, a bottle of water in his hand, perspiration breaking out over his forehead, his stomach muscles contracting and relaxing in cadence with his breath. Pouring the cool water over his face seemed like a better possibility for the liquid refreshment. Louie kept an eye on him while shuffling through some official looking papers.

"You okay?" he asked after a few minutes.

Nash tried to take a deep breath, but his lungs refused to expand. Instead, he nodded in response to Louie's question.

"How?"

Nash didn't recognize his own voice.

Louie cleared his throat.

"Shot. Drowned. They're not sure yet which came first."

Bending over in the chair, Nash desperately fought the urge to vomit. Gina Woods dead? The vivacious so-alive Gina Woods? He could hardly believe the words, but he had seen the body lying still in the cold morgue.

"Family know?" he uttered.

"Called you first," Louie answered. "Getting ready to call them now."

Nash nodded, once again unable to form intelligible words. Louie seemed to understand and found the appropriate telephone numbers to call. Nash's ears heard the conversation and surmised Cliff had been the one to answer the phone, but his own ears rang with such force that Louie's words seemed to emanate from a place far away from reality.

He didn't know how long he'd sat there, but at some point he began to trust his legs once more to carry him to his car and then made his way to the familiar and comforting surroundings of family.

———————————•◉•———————————

Sitting once again at his desk, staring at the group of photos on the wall, Nash considered which person in Gina's life would want to kill her. First wife, Tammy Woods? He'd seen no animosity or resentment there. Cliff? Not as long as he had an interest in Gina. But what if she had found out about his gambling debt and threatened to expose his weakness? Perhaps that would be enough reason for a struggle or confrontation. Candy? She sure didn't waste any love on her stepmother, but she hardly spent time in the same room with her. Lindy? Lindy was off on some place in Europe which eliminated her entirely from the list of suspects at this point. Susan? Doubt it. Susan just continued to be mad at herself and the world in general. Greg Carter? Her lover? Probably not unless the affair had become stagnant or threatening in some way. Zoe Carter? Possibly, but Nash thought Zoe preferred just drowning her misery with liquor. The list of suspects all seemed unlikely.

Louie called with the results of the autopsy. Apparently Gina had been shot, probably while she had been swimming in the family pool at the house on Hickory Lane. No gun had been found. No signs of a struggle. The body had been found by Horace, the butler, who had immediately called the authorities. All the children had been contacted.

Taking his gun from its place in the drawer, he started for the office door. Nash needed some fresh air.

Chapter 12

Katie and Nash sat on a park bench. No picnic lunch. No lively chatter. Both had been stunned by the news.

"But...who?" Katie was saying. "Who would do such a thing?"

Still Nash found it difficult to talk about it.

"I can tell you are really struggling with this. What bothers you most, Nash?" Katie asked, aware of the depth of emotion Nash was experiencing.

Once again Nash felt his insides in turmoil.

"I've been thinking. Is it possible that I have caused it?" he answered. "Did Gina Woods die because I baited Greg Carter by using Sam?"

"I don't know a lot," she soothed, "but I seriously doubt that is the reason behind it. Blaming yourself is not the answer nor will it help in solving this case."

She was right of course.

He turned to her with hurt in his eyes and he spoke softly.

"I was just wondering if anything had been said around the office," he spoke.

"Everything's been pretty quiet since the news of Gina Woods' death. Mr. Carter has been holed up in his office with instructions that he's not be bothered. The atmosphere is really subdued, like gloom and doom has descended over the entire complex, like we're all operating in a vacuum. First Mr. Woods and now the second Mrs. Woods."

They sat watching pigeons as they scavenged for morsels of food left behind by other visitors.

"One more thing," Katie added. "The word is that the first Mrs. Woods is to be in the office by the end of the week. Maybe something about her having some say-so in the company now that Mr. Woods is gone?"

Nash quietly shook his head. That made sense with what he knew about the terms of the will.

Katie felt his emotion and placed her hand on top of his in a comforting manner.

"You'll figure it out," she whispered.

Again Nash shook his head in agreement. It was just that right now he didn't know where to turn.

He absentmindedly tapped his pencil on the surface of the desk. Gina's funeral was a simple one with little fuss, one that Nash learned was paid for by Tammy Woods. Well, she certainly had the finances to do that; and given what Nash had seen of her, it would fit that she would be compassionate enough do such a thing. And apparently Gina Woods had no family. At least none had shown up for the funeral. The four Woods children had made courtesy appearances and Greg and Zoe Carter were there, interesting enough not together. Nash and Louie had stood at the edge of the group of mourners.

As Nash sat studying the photos on his office wall, the door suddenly opened. Nash had a visitor.

"Good morning," came the female voice that jarred him from his thoughts.

Nash straightened in his chair.

"I'm sorry," he apologized. "I didn't hear your knock."

"That's because I didn't," came the reply as his guest deposited a brown suitcase near the door.

She was older, but remarkably attractive. Gray hair, cut short, curled around her face, a face which appeared to be fairly free of wrinkles. Gray eyes...eyes that seemed familiar...crinkled at the corners when she spoke and he noticed that in spite of her age, she was shapely. She was smartly dressed in a beige pantsuit with a green and brown patterned blouse; and although her shoes were a low heel, they were fashionable.

"How can I help you?" Nash asked as he stood and offered his hand.

Her handshake was firm and business like.

"I understand you're the young man investigating the murder of Stephen Woods."

"That's correct. And you are...?"

"I am Margaret Shore Hastings, grandmother to the four spoiled grandchildren."

"And Tammy's mother," she added as means of clarification in answer to the blank look on Nash's face. "And I'm here to help straighten out this mess. Got in this morning from Italy and came directly here."

Nash studied the face. Yes, the gray eyes were similar to Tammy's, but they were not near as soft. Nash didn't know whether to be offended or grateful for the offer.

"I don't recall seeing you at Stephen's funeral," he questioned.

"I was on a trip up in the mountains at the time and couldn't be reached. I only heard about it after the fact."

After Nash studied the woman, he was convinced she was probably telling the truth. This was a woman who enjoyed adventure. Perhaps Lindy had inherited those genes.

"How is it that you intend to help?" he fumbled.

Taking a seat on the edge of the desk, she looked him square in the eyes.

"I know this family pretty well," she said. "I can ferret out any inconsistencies, any secrets lurking around that the average person might overlook. Not that I'm calling you average. You appear to be a quite capable young man. But I've been around long enough to be devious. As a matter of fact, I've worked hard to get that reputation."

She smiled a clever smile.

"I'll be staying at The Gateway," she said as she stood from her resting place on the edge of the desk. "I'll be in touch."

With that remark, she extended her hand and started for the door. Picking up the handle to her suitcase, she stopped to survey the room.

"We need to do something about your office space. And these stairs are a killer!"

Part way through the door, she stopped again.

"Oops! Sorry about that. Under the circumstances, *killer* might have been an inappropriate choice of words."

Once again humor spread across her face and Nash stood with a look of bewilderment on his. What had just blown through his office?

"Who was that?" Anne Meijer asked as she came through the office door carrying an old wooden chair.

"So you met Margaret Shore Hastings, have you? That's Tammy Woods' mother."

Anne closed the door behind her after giving one more wide-eyed look down the stairway.

"She's an elegant looking woman."

"And a very forceful one, I think," Nash replied.

Anne stood near the door, still not entirely comfortable with entering the room Nash called his office.

"Oh, here's a chair I found in Papa's storeroom. I thought you might be able to use it. I think it has character."

Nash nodded his head and smiled.

She cautiously sat the chair near the door.

"How are you?" she asked shyly.

Nash shuffled through some papers on his desk.

"I'm okay," he murmured, not willing to look Anne in the face. "Just a part of the job."

Anne thought for a moment, listening carefully to what she perceived as depression in Nash's comment.

"Not a particularly pleasant part of the job," she said softly.

Nash didn't answer.

"I'll just be going," she said and turned to reach for the door handle.

"No. No, don't go," Nash pleaded. "I'd really enjoy your company for a while. Sit down."

Anne slid into the chair she'd just put down.

"Tell me about your classes," Nash began. "How are they going? And what about the paper you're writing?"

"Classes are going good. I may get all A's this grade period."

Nash was not surprised at that. He'd thought all along that Anne was probably a good student.

"And I've turned in the first draft of the first part of my paper and my teacher said it was probably one of the more interesting papers he's read in a long time. We won't actually turn the final copy in now until the fall semester."

Nash smiled with satisfaction. Anne was doing a good job with the paper.

Anne's eyes lit up as she shared her teachers' comments. The shy Anne came alive when she was telling him about her paper and the things she had included, things about Nash and the personal investigation business.

"My friend down at the precinct offered for me to look through the mug shots for the photo of the guy with Lindy Woods."

"I could do that!" she was excited. Then thinking it over, she quickly added, "That is, if that would be okay. I mean, if he would let me do that. I mean, do you have to be a Private Investigator or something in order to do that?"

Nash smiled.

"I think it's something you could do. But it's boring," he added. "I can check with Louie to make sure if you want."

"Yes. I'd like to do that."

Once again Nash saw that spark when she talked about helping.

"You still think you'd like to be a PI?" he asked.

Anne considered the possibilities.

"Yes," she answered. "I see how you help people and you care about people. I like that."

Nash swallowed.

"Yeah, the key is not to care too much."

Anne smiled.

Realizing Nash was talking about himself, she added, "I think that quality just makes you a better investigator."

They both were dripping with sweat from their early morning run. It didn't happen very often these days what with Nash busy with the Woods murder and Louie being swamped with cases, including the death of Gina Woods. Wiping a small towel across his face, Louie offered a bottle of water to Nash.

"I know we're getting close to wrapping this case up," he said. "I have a gut feeling."

Nash wanted to ask what that was, but wondered if he even wanted to know.

"That's been pretty accurate in the past," Nash offered.

"Yeah, but it takes facts to make a conviction. Small caliber gun. One a woman could use."

"That could fit a lot of people. And there are several who use the gun range for target practice. I've already looked into that. Susan Woods, Greg Carter, Zoe Carter and who else is anyone's guess. Maybe even Candy Woods. I'd hate to think she could have a gun in her hands. You think it was a woman?"

"I'd stake my career on it. Beautiful woman. Can be a threat to a lot of other women."

Nash took a long drink from the water bottle, thinking about how beautiful Gina Woods was...had been.

"I have a young girl who is shadowing me for a school paper. Do you think she could come down and go through some books to see if she can match that photo to a mug shot?"

"Sure. We could do that. Send her down. Did you tell her how boring that can be?"

Nash smiled.

"Well, she wants to know what it's like to be a personal investigator so I guess she'll find out. I've told her it isn't all that glamorous. If you don't mind, I can send her down after she gets out of school."

"Fine by me," Louie said. "You cooled off enough?"

"Yeah," Nash answered, finishing the last of the bottle of water.

It was time for both of them to get back to work.

Anne showed up at the precinct every day after school and was so quiet, Louie almost forgot to tell her it was time for his shift to be over. Tucked away in a corner of the busy room, she patiently looked through each page of the endless books of photos and compared each to the picture of the man dressed in black, the man who had met Lindy Woods at the marina restaurant. By the end of day three, she'd hit pay dirt. The man dressed in black had been arrested several times in connection with mob activities but allegations had never been proven. When Louie pulled up the paperwork, Anne was quick to sort out Raoul's name.

"Amazing," Nash complimented.

Anne beamed with delight.

"Good work, Anne. Your diligence has paid off. One more piece of the puzzle."

"I enjoyed it," she said. "And you are right. Yes, just like working on a giant jigsaw puzzle. Never quite sure where the piece fits until you put them all together."

While Anne had been working on the photo, Nash was following the activities of the Woods family and those at the offices of Woods and Carter. According to Katie, Greg Carter had pretty much been confined to the offices and Zoe Carter had made two unannounced emotional appearances there. And Nash had been invited to lunch at The Gateway with Grandmother Margaret Shore Hastings.

Chapter 13

As Nash walked into the restaurant/bar area of The Gateway, he had flashbacks of his time there the night he made a visit to floor #11 and found out about Cliff Woods' gambling problem. The restaurant took on a whole different atmosphere in the light of day. Just as he was asked about seating, he saw Margaret waving at him from a nearby table. Even at her age, she seemed to command the room.

"So good of you to come," she said graciously as she extended her hand.

Merely shaking her hand seemed to cause a flow of energy. This was one powerful woman.

"Thank you for the invitation," he responded. "What can I do for you?"

"The first thing you can do is decide what you'd like for lunch," she answered abruptly, picking up the menu and scanning the selections herself.

She placed it back on the table almost as quickly as she'd picked it up.

"Of course, there's nothing like a home cooked meal, is there, Nash? I figure you are a home cooked meal type of guy."

Once again picking up the menu, she confessed.

"I've never been much of a cook," she admitted. "Just never was my thing. Now, my daughter, she's quite the cook."

Nash nodded in agreement, remembering the afternoon he'd spent with Tammy Woods at her home in a Detroit suburb.

They had neared the end of their meal before she spoke about anything pertaining to the case.

"I've taken care of Cliff's problem," she blurted out. "And I've talked with him and I hope he's learned his lesson. Don't think he'll be bothered now the debt is paid. But I intend to keep close tabs on that situation. He won't want to come up against his grandmother's wrath again. And although he was in hock quite a bit, I see no connection between that and the murders. If there ever was an interest between Cliff and Gina, it was slight. I'm convinced of that. Just as I am convinced she was involved with someone other than Stephen. Merely my opinion. Everybody knows he put his work first. And that's probably what happened there. That's why Tammy left him, you know."

Well, that certainly was blunt and to the point, something Nash was beginning to expect from Grandmother Margaret.

Nash wasn't sure how he was to respond.

"Don't worry. I won't keep any secrets from you. I'm pretty much up front with what I do and say as you may already have observed."

Oh, yes, Nash had observed that alright.

"Speaking of Tammy," he began, "what are your feelings about Raoul?"

He saw her slight hesitation, but she quickly recovered and forged ahead.

"Don't care much for him myself. Do not understand what she sees in him. After all, my daughter is an intelligent and beautiful woman. She does not have to settle for anything less than she wants. But I also know that she loved Stephen very much and I don't think she will ever get over him. Have you experienced that kind of a relationship, Nash?"

Nash swallowed hard. He hadn't expected the conversation to turn personal. But he was just learning that Margaret Shore Hastings would never be predictable.

"No," he faltered. "I guess I haven't."

"Well," Margaret said in a matter of fact manner, "I hope you do some day. Everyone should have that experience."

Her statement caused Nash to briefly consider what part of her past could have evoked that response.

Margaret was picking up the check and moved to stand.

"And I hope it will be an experience that will last forever for you."

Nash struggled for conversation.

"What about Candy?" he asked.

Margaret hesitated.

"What about Candy?" she repeated.

"Anything she might be hiding?"

A shadow came over Margaret's face.

"Candy's a lot like me," she said. "Pretty much up front with what we think."

"You must be close to her," he ventured.

"We've spent a lot of time together."

And she was off to pay the tab. Lunch conversation was over.

"Susan's next," she called over her shoulder. I'll be in touch."

Somehow Nash pitied Susan once Grandma Margaret got hold of her.

———————————◆●●————————————

Midge was putting a selection of blouses on a rack at the dress shop. It had been a fairly quiet morning in the store. She enjoyed her work of unpacking, tagging and hanging merchandise and helping women who frequented the store. Regular customers had learned to respect the judgment of the friendly clerk in matters of style and fashion. And Midge knew her customers, at least the ones who were regulars. She knew which women had upcoming special occasions and made sure suitable items were available and in stock in the store. She knew when school dances were scheduled and made sure items were ordered that would appeal to teenagers. And, Mrs. Hanover, her boss, knew what a gem she had in Midge. Yes, Midge Adams was good at her job.

Although regular customers were like family, new customers were always welcome as well. Midge looked up from her work as the tinkling sound of the bell on the door announced the arrival of possible buyers.

She'd never seen these potential customers before. Three girls. One with attractive auburn hair, one with dark hair and one with hair of assorted colors. Midge welcomed them and let them look through the merchandise, noticing what items seemed to interest each one. Midge's knack for noticing detail made her a good sales person. She let them browse for quite a long period of time.

"I'd like to try these on," the girl with the auburn hair said as she approached with an armful of clothes.

"Right this way."

And Midge led the way to the dressing rooms.

"Is there anything in particular that you might be looking for?" she asked. "Something I might be able to help you find?"

The girl with the auburn hair answered her.

"Anything that's unique and different," she said. "I'm in the mood for different."

The girl with the auburn hair and the dark headed girl both made several selections and went to the dressing rooms to see if they did indeed look as good on as they had on the hangers. The multi-colored hair girl was engrossed at the jewelry counter. Although Jan, the second clerk in the store was there, she was busy with unpacking, so Midge thought perhaps she should keep an eye on things out front. After watching for a period of time, she was fairly comfortable that the girl with the multi-colored hair was not a threat. It was then Midge thought of some new merchandise that had recently arrived. Certainly fit the bill for unique and different. Guessing at the size, she selected several items and started toward the dressing rooms. She stopped short when she heard the conversation between the two girls.

"So your grandmother is in town. That must be a drag."

Laughter.

"Not necessarily. You haven't met my grandmother."

"Really."

"Yeah, really. She's quite the unconventional grandmother. Spends most of her time abroad. Only visits once in a while. But let me tell you, those visits are filled with a lot of activity...shopping, prying, opinions. Oh, yes, things are never dull when Grandmother Margaret is in town!"

"Sounds interesting. I know you're close to her after spending those months with her in Europe?"

"Sometimes I feel close to her, but then she's gone again. But I know she has obligations overseas and for that I am grateful."

Pause.

"Girl, I really feel for you."

Pause.

"Candy, you need to talk to someone. You can't go on like this. Maybe you just need to go ahead and tell your mother?"

Silence.

"Blackmail is nothing to take lightly, girl. You simply cannot just handle this on your own. You still don't want to go to the police?"

"No," she was emphatic. "No police. I have to protect..."

Midge had not intended to eavesdrop on their conversation. Clearing her throat, she made her presence known.

"Ladies, I have some things here you might want to consider," she suggested.

Handing them over the top of the dressing room door, she turned to leave.

"Thank you, miss."

"You're very welcome," Midge answered and went back to the sales floor.

The girls took their time in making selections and finally the girl with the auburn hair placed a mountain of items on the counter next to the check out. This would be a good sales day in the little shop.

"I'll take these," she stated.

"Good choices," Midge answered as she began to remove the items from the hangers, impressed with the quantity of selected merchandise.

"Oh, I think this is a really cute top," she observed. "We have a necklace that would look great with this. Would you like to see it?"

The girls exchanged glances.

"Sure. Why not?"

From there, several pieces of jewelry were added to the items of clothing to be purchased.

"You have a real eye for fashion," the dark haired girl commented.

Midge smiled.

"Thank you."

Midge totaled the purchases and presented the girl with the auburn hair with the amount who in turn placed a credit card on the counter. Midge glanced at the name on the card and her senses became heightened. Candy Woods. Hadn't she heard that name from Nash's murder case? Trying hard not to react, she handed the credit card with the receipt to the young lady and forced her best smile.

"Thank you, Miss Woods," she said. "You got some really good bargains today. I hope you'll visit us again."

"We will," Candy said as she picked up her packages. "This is a really cool place."

"Thank you," Midge said as she watched the girls exit the shop and attempted to take a deep breath.

"Whatever is the matter with you, Midge?" Ma asked. "You are as nervous as a long tailed cat in a room full of rocking chairs."

"Anxious to talk to Nash," Midge answered. "He is planning on being here for supper, right?"

"As far as I know," Ma said, handing Midge a stack of plates. "Here, doing something helpful will make the time go faster."

Midge finished setting the table.

"Was that Nash's car in the driveway?" Midge was at the window.

"Land sakes, Midge, just go out there and see."

Midge raced to the driveway, arriving just as Nash opened the car door.

"Hey, what's up, little sister?" he said, reaching for his jacket lying beside him.

"Oh, Nash," she bubbled, "I think one of your suspects was in the store today."

"Well, as far as I know, they're free to go where they want. Buy anything?"

"Yes, a lot as a matter of fact, but..."

"There's more?" Nash asked.

"Well, yes," she paused. "I overheard some conversation. I wasn't eavesdropping or anything. I was just taking some items back to the dressing rooms for them to try and I couldn't help but overhear what was being said."

"Whoa, slow down here. Just which one of my suspects are we talking about here?"

"Candy. Candy Woods. She and her friends were in the shop today."

"So did she buy something?" Nash asked as he continued removing his briefcase from the car.

"Well, yes, as a matter of fact, she bought a lot of things, but that's not what I want to tell you."

"What, then?"

She had his attention.

"There's more?"

"Blackmail. One of the girls she was with indicated she was being blackmailed. Candy, that is. I really wasn't trying to eavesdrop."

"Hold on," Nash interrupted. "Start at the beginning."

Midge took a deep breath.

"Three girls came into the shop. A girl with auburn hair, one with dark hair and one with all different colors."

Nash had vivid pictures of the girls from the library in his mind.

"Two of the girls...not the one with the streaks in her hair...went into the dressing room to try on clothes and I was taking some other items for them to try when I heard it.

"I distinctly heard the word blackmail and that she shouldn't try to handle it on her own and she still didn't want to go to the police. I think it was the dark headed girl who spoke so it was the auburn girl who is in trouble. And then when she made the purchases, she used her credit card and her name was right there...Candy Woods."

Midge stopped to take a breath.

Nash was more than interested now.

"Ah, interesting. Thanks, Midge," he said. "That's another piece of the puzzle. I just need to find out where it fits."

Seeing Midge was still shaken by her experience, Nash put his arm around her shoulder and they walked into the house and to Ma's supper table where a hot meal and good conversation would once again be the norm.

Chapter 14

———————●◐●———————

Zoe Carter backed her SUV out of the three-car garage. A headscarf and a pair of sunglasses masked her face. She was dressed for the gym, feeling the need to work off some nervous energy. It had been several nights since she had been able to sleep; and when she did, sleep was filled with dark images. And eating had been pretty much out of the question. The liquor cabinet had been her salvation...or so she thought. The truth was that Zoe Carter was not thinking clearly at all. Placing a plastic bag beside her in the passenger seat, she threw an upscale duffle bag into the back seat.

Checking her surroundings more than once, she eased the champagne colored SUV into the street of the exclusive neighborhood. These homes were located on the hill overlooking the rest of the city as if they were asserting their superiority of wealth and prestige over those less fortunate from their lofty location. Was she being followed? That feeling had been a constant since...well, it had been a constant. A car behind her at the stop sign honked; and jerking nervously in response, she moved cautiously forward. She needed to take a deep breath; but, just like sleep, that seemed another impossibility.

Greg. How long had she shared a house with a man she hardly recognized anymore? He had gone one direction; she had gone another. Greg was as distant as a man could possibly be. And secretive. He'd sheltered her from personal business under the excuse that she didn't need to worry about such things. Now she wondered what other secrets he was hiding. Lately he seemed to be nervous and on edge, especially since Stephen's death. What did he suspect?

How stupid she had been to have not confronted him when she first found out about Gina. How stupid he had been to not realize she indeed knew about his affair with Gina Woods. And that had hurt. Her stomach muscles contracted at the thought. Not only had she been suspicious of his activity with Gina, but she couldn't get rid of the thought that he might somehow be involved in Stephen's death.

After all, with Stephen gone, it would be more or less clear sailing for Greg and Gina. Zoe certainly would not stand in their way. Not anymore. Those thoughts had long since disappeared from her mind. Angry? Yes. Bitter? Yes. Embarrassed? Yes. Tears no longer came to her eyes. Those had dried up a long time ago as had her love for her husband, perhaps replaced with hatred. Maybe she hadn't been the wife he expected. Was he the man she once dreamed of? But she didn't deserve the humiliation either. And didn't everyone know of his indiscretions?

She had followed him herself to the Blue Star Motel where she had watched in agony, visualizing what might have been taking place within the confines of the room. She had considered confronting them, but could not endure those consequences. But that problem had been resolved with Gina's death. Zoe hadn't counted on other problems surfacing.

Louie asked Nash to ride along with him on this particular day since he had shared an interest in the case. They watched from a safe distance as the champagne SUV made its way across town. Suspicions had risen as more information poured in about Gina's death.

"Nothing any worse than a love triangle," Louie repeated as he shook his head. "Messy."

Nash still had twinges thinking about the lovely Gina's body lying cold in the morgue.

"You okay?" Louie asked.

"Yeah. Yeah, sure," came the unsteady answer.

Louie glanced at Nash sitting in the passenger seat of the detective's car. Nash was learning a lot on this case...some difficult lessons, the most important of which was that of distancing himself from the persons involved.

"You got any more leads?" he asked, attempting to divert Nash's thoughts.

"Candy Woods was in Midge's store the other day," he shared. "Midge overheard some conversation about possible blackmail. I've been trying to come up with any reason Candy Woods would have information worth someone's time to blackmail her."

"Another family member?" Louie asked.

"I've thought about that," Nash answered. "Nothing as of yet."

"Look," he said, gesturing out the window. "Mrs. Carter is turning into the gym."

They watched as the SUV slowed, stopped and proceeded to move to the back of the building.

"What the heck?" Louie spouted.

He drove off to the side and found a spot behind the seclusion of a pickup truck in an effort not to be seen as they observed the activity.

Zoe Carter pulled the champagne colored SUV next to the gym's dumpster; and getting out of the car with plastic bag in hand, she threw it into the dumpster. Looking around and apparently not noticing the car parked behind the pickup truck, she returned to the SUV and drove to the front of the building where she retrieved the duffle bag from the back seat and entered the gym through the front doors.

Louie looked at Nash.

"You know what comes next, don't you?" he said.

"Yeah," Nash answered as he reached for the door handle.

Together they made their way to the dumpster where Louie retrieved the plastic bag. Opening it revealed a small caliber gun.

"I think we're close to solving one of these murders," Louie announced to Nash as he radioed for back up.

"Protocol," he said. "I don't expect any trouble, but one never knows. Best to be prepared."

Minutes later a patrol car rolled into the parking lot and Louie and Nash went into action. Zoe Carter had not left the building.

"I don't expect any trouble," Louie repeated to the officers. "But you never know."

There was no trouble. Zoe appeared to be almost relieved when she saw the men approaching her.

"We have reason to believe that this is your gun, Mrs. Carter. Of course we'll check it for fingerprints."

"It's mine," she freely admitted. "I should have killed them both."

She went peacefully, tired of the pretense, tired of the guilt, tired of the hatred, tired of keeping the secret.

"You moving, Nash?" Mr. Meijer asked as Nash entered the front door of the delicatessen.

"Me? Me moving? No," a bewildered Nash answered. "Why do you ask?"

"I see lots of boxes. Coming, going."

Nash frowned and started for the stairs that led to his office. Sure enough, boxes were stacked in the hallway.

"What's going on here?" he asked.

A man dressed in delivery clothes removed a pencil from behind his ear; and taking a clip board, prepared to have Nash sign for the delivery.

"But I haven't ordered anything," he protested.

"Hey, buddy, all I know is this stuff was to be delivered to this address. I just deliver."

"Perhaps I can explain," the voice came from down the steps.

Nash turned to see Margaret Shore Hastings, dressed in a bright blue suit, making her way up the stairs.

"Open the door, Nash. I've ordered just a few things to make this office look more like an office. Or at least to create a different atmosphere, one that will reflect your profession."

She paused as she looked into Nash's stunned face.

"Well, go ahead. Let's get this show on the road."

"But..." Nash began.

Holding up her hand to silence him, she shook her head.

"No refusals," she smiled. "I like to do things for people I like. And I like you, Nash."

Nash fumbled for the key while the delivery men looked on.

In the next few moments and under the direction of Margaret Shore Hastings, a table and chairs and file cabinet and a new desk chair on rollers and a computer with printer along with a stock of paper and pens and other desk supplies were all put in place. Yet to be unpacked was a rather large aquarium.

"But I don't need an aquarium," Nash protested.

"Nonsense. It will calm your nerves in stressful times," she said as she continued adding water to the aquarium and then dumped in several goldfish from little white containers.

Hanging a valence at the window and placing a series of framed pictures on the wall and plopping a potted plant on the new desk, she stood back to survey her decorating skills.

"There now," she said. "That looks a lot better."

Nash was speechless.

Grandmother Hastings started for the door.

Turning, she said, "No need to thank me."

"Oh, yeah, thanks."

She paused again.

"I don't know much more, but I've heard some rumors about some blackmailing going on within the family."

And she was gone.

Nash looked around the room. Maybe it did look a little better.

Anne knocked on the doorframe of the open door.

"What happened here?" she asked, noticing all the changes that had been made.

Nash rubbed his hand over his head.

"Margaret Shore Hastings," he answered.

Chapter 15

It was difficult to read the emotion in Greg Carter's face as his wife was being led from the courtroom. Zoe Carter appeared to be resigned to her fate, perhaps even relieved, maybe an easier choice than to live with the humiliation. The facts were clear. The murder weapon was registered to Zoe Carter. Testimony revealed fingerprints on the gun indeed belonged to Zoe Carter. She had deliberately gone to the Woods' home on Hickory Lane with the intention of doing harm to Gina Woods.

Greg Carter declined questions from the press as he pushed his way through the crowd. Nash followed Greg after he left the proceedings, followed him as he drove to the house on the hill, emerged with a package, got back in his vehicle and drove to the river where he threw the package in the water. He stood for some time staring into the murkiness of the water as it swirled below him before he got in his car and drove away. Nash's cell phone was in his hand with Louie's number on speed dial.

Divers exploring the area the following day came up empty.

With Gina's death resolved, Nash devoted his time concentrating on Candy…Candy's secret.

"It's great to see you, Nash," Margaret welcomed as she opened the door to her lush penthouse apartment at The Gateway. "Come in, won't you?"

"I won't stay long," Nash said as he stepped through the doorway. "I just have a couple of questions."

"Any way I can help."

His questions were vague, but he found out what he wanted to know. Candy Woods had spent six months with Grandmother Margaret Shore Hastings in Europe in her small but high end villa. He had a place and he had dates. Unknowingly, he had gotten the information he was searching for.

Researching the small village revealed that it was located at the foot of the mountains on a strip of land between the mountains and the seashore, a beautiful setting against the scenic mountain area with its plentiful supply of green trees and shrubs, temperature moderated by the ocean. A little farming, a little fishing, a little tourist trade. Yachts of the wealthy were frequently seen moored in the docks. It was a very small town, less than six hundred people, but it did have two churches and a small hospital run by the local nuns. Nash began by placing a phone call to one of the two churches.

"My name is Nash Adams and I am calling from the states to inquire about someone who may have been in your parish about eighteen months to two years ago. Do you speak English?"

It was broken English at best. But the priest was gracious enough to take the time to check records and came back with the answer that he did not remember a young lady with auburn hair in the suggested time frame and did not know anyone by the name of Margaret Shore Hastings and could not find anyone by that name in the church registry.

A second call to the second church was a bit more successful. Father John did know of Margaret Shore Hastings; and although she was not a regular attendee at mass, he did remember an infant she had brought for christening some months ago.

Nash knew what his next call would be. It took a little convincing with the nun in charge of the hospital to establish that a girl using the name of Meg Shore, an interesting combination of names, had given birth to a baby girl during that time frame. Candy's secret was becoming clearer now. Spending six months with Grandmother Hastings in Europe had been the shield to cover up a pregnancy. But what did that have to do with blackmailing? Someone must have found out about the baby and was blackmailing Candy? But who?

Grandmother Hastings answered his knock on the door of the plush apartment at The Gateway.

"Nash, I wasn't expecting to see you this evening," she appeared surprised.

She was dressed in a flowing dressing gown of a pale yellow color and clearly hadn't been expecting guests.

"I've come at a bad time," Nash apologized. "I could come back another time."

"Nonsense," she put his mind at ease. "You obviously have news."

"I've uncovered a piece of information I want to share with you," he began. "May I come in?"

"Surely," she said, stepping aside. "Please do."

He sat uncomfortably on the sofa, staring at the coffee table before him, hoping he would feel more comfortable by the time he left the apartment. She sat across from him, intent on whatever had brought him to her suite at this hour of the evening.

"Coffee?" she offered.

"No, thank you," he declined.

"What is it, Nash?" she asked. "What's troubling you?"

"I've made some long distance phone calls," he began. "To this little town in Europe..."

He let his words sink in, closely watching Margaret's face for some kind of reaction.

"I think you know it well. I talked with Father John and then I called the small hospital there to speak with Sister Rose Marie."

Grandmother Hastings sat back in her chair with a sigh.

"You know?" she asked as she peered at him over her glasses.

"I think I do. I think I've put the pieces together. Correct me if I'm wrong. Candy was pregnant; and in order for her to keep it a secret from her family and spare them the humiliation, she turned to her grandmother living in Europe, the grandmother who took her in."

A second sigh escaped Margaret's mouth. Sooner or later the secret had to be revealed.

"Yes, you are correct. She couldn't tell her parents. And the boy, well, he wasn't anyone the family would approve of. An indiscretion. Besides, with the divorce and Stephen's remarriage, Candy was pretty confused about things. It was a really difficult time for my granddaughter. She came to me out of desperation and I was glad I could be there for her."

"Where is the child now if I may ask?"

Margaret nodded her head. No need to keep the details from Nash.

119

"A couple I know of...a really nice couple...are caring for her, with the possibility of adoption. But Candy can visit any time she wants. And she has...visited, that is. Those visits are very emotional, but the adoptive parents want the child to know her biological mother. And, of course, I see the little sweetheart frequently."

"The part I do not understand is who would want to blackmail her about the child?"

Margaret Shore Hastings' eyes widened.

"I don't know anything about blackmailing. Oh, poor Candy. She's been through so much. I know. She's a bit wild and opinionated, but she is a sweet and caring girl. I certainly hope you're wrong about that blackmailing part, Mr. Adams."

"The word was overheard in a conversation Candy had with a friend and I have reason to believe the source is accurate."

He preferred not to let Margaret know that his source was his own sister, Midge.

"Oh, my! This is an interesting development. The poor child has had too many secrets to hide. But who?"

Nash shook his head.

"I don't know, but I need to find out. Somehow I feel as if it all may fit together to answer the question of who murdered Stephen Woods. I haven't figured that out yet. But how well do you know Greg Carter? Would he be capable of doing something like this?"

"Oh, I don't know. I really don't know him that well. I just get negative vibrations when I'm around the man."

She paused with real concern on her face.

"Will Candy's secret become public knowledge?" she asked.

"Not if I can help it," Nash concurred. "It's not my place to judge other people...unless it applies directly to someone's guilt or innocence."

Margaret nodded in agreement and relief. She wanted to spare Candy any more stress.

Nash was picking up Katie to go to a movie and he was running late. For three days now he had tailed Greg Carter. Of interest were his trips to the cemetery where he visited the grave of Gina Woods. Not once had he visited his wife in prison. Greg had met once again with Susan Woods and that left Nash wondering what of importance the two of them had to discuss. He watched as Greg continued his routine of target practice at the range, kept business appointments, kept meetings with his attorney and met with Tammy Woods...all of which seemed to be perfectly normal, at least on the surface.

Katie was waiting for him when he pulled up in front of her house. Katie was so easy to be with and full of life and on occasion, informative. Today was no exception.

"Hey, why so quiet?" she asked after several minutes of silence riding in the car.

"Just lost in thought, I guess," he replied.

"The murder case, I suppose?"

"Yes. Lots of complications; no solutions," he admitted.

They continued in silence.

"Well, perhaps this is of some significance," she began. "The first Mrs. Woods has been in the office and it seems she wants to take an active part in the business and that has Mr. Carter in a dither. I don't know if he feels threatened by that or just simply does not like her or what, but he has been really irritable and jumpy lately."

Should he share his suspicions with Katie? He decided to chance it.

"Do you think Greg Carter could have murdered his partner, Stephen Woods?"

There it was, finally verbalized, the thought that had been playing around in his mind for over a week now.

Instead of the shock or surprise he expected, she answered calmly.

"I have to admit that I have had the same feelings. And every time he walks anywhere close to my desk, I get this funny sensation like something awful is about to happen."

"Really? Interesting you should say that. Seems like I've heard that recently from someone else."

Nash sat in the movie, staring at the screen, aware of Katie in the seat next to him, tasting the popcorn they shared; but at the end of the evening, he couldn't repeat any of the movie plot. His mind had been elsewhere.

Since Nash had literally made no progress in his surveillance of Susan, he decided that perhaps the best approach was to confront things headlong. He knew where to find Susan Woods at lunchtime. And he was right. Susan Woods was having lunch at the Easy Skillet and luckily there was no one sitting opposite her. Pulling out the chair, he noticed the astonished look on Susan's face.

"Is this chair taken?" he asked.

Putting down the menu with some degree of disgust, she flashed her dark eyes at him.

"Mr. Adams, are you ever going to leave my family alone?" she asked.

"Whenever I find your father's murderer," he replied. "Now may I please sit down?"

"I suppose. You do look rather awkward standing there."

With that, Nash slid into the chair across the table from Susan while Susan continued perusing the menu and ignoring him. This was not going to be easy.

Nash cleared his throat, hoping perhaps that would engage her in conversation. She continued to ignore him.

"What's good for lunch here?" he initiated.

When she didn't respond, he tried a second time.

"I know you eat here almost every day so you're probably familiar with the menu choices."

Again, the menu in Susan's hand came down hard on the table.

"Look, I said you could sit down. That does not mean I have to make polite table conversation with you!" she was beyond firm.

What had Nash ever done to her to deserve such contempt? Then he remembered her intense dislike she'd had for men since her parents' divorce.

Nash also put his menu on the table. Perhaps it was never going to work to be polite to this woman.

"No, you don't. And I am through being polite as well. I am here on business and was trying to make it as pleasant as possible, but let me get directly to the point. And then you can have your lunch in peace and I can go about the business of finding the person who murdered your father. Or do you not care about that either? Are you so cold and calloused that you don't care about anyone anymore except yourself?"

His manner had become agitated and his voice had raised in volume significantly. Susan Woods look startled, just as if she'd never been talked to in that manner ever before. And maybe she hadn't. She was living in a world where everything and everybody had to be politically correct as well as subtle and devious.

Nash continued.

"I don't have time to waste on handling people with kid gloves, particularly those who are rude and self-centered. Now may I ask you some questions that might help in finding the killer...your father's killer?"

Susan's entire attitude changed on the spot. Putting her menu aside and placing her forearms on the table, she stared directly into his challenging eyes.

"Yes, Mr. Adams," she said softly, "I do wish to help in any way I can to find out who murdered my father."

Now it was Nash's turn to be startled. All this woman really needed was someone to be as strong as she appeared to be. The atmosphere suddenly became more relaxed.

"Good," he said. "Now then, what is your association with Greg Carter?"

"Greg Carter is courting me to move up the ladder in the company. He thinks I would be a great asset."

"Has he made any inappropriate advances towards you?"

She laughed.

"We're talking about Greg Carter here," she said. "Greg comes on to every woman. I think his interest in Gina was just to get back at my Dad."

"Why is that?"

"Greg has always been jealous of my Dad. I think it goes back to their college days. I don't know for sure, but I always suspected they both wanted to marry my mother. And my Dad won out."

The questions and answers flew back and forth. His questions were direct as were her answers. Susan was not sold on the idea of moving up the ladder in the company, mostly because she had not completely decided whether or not Greg Carter could be trusted. Then there was the fact that her mother would have controlling interest in the company since Stephen had left everything to her. And Susan was positive she wanted the position because she deserved it, not as part of some controlling interest on Greg Carter's part.

Nash had reached the end of his questioning and the rapid fire of questions and answers slowed. They both sat back and relaxed.

Susan smiled.

"The potato soup here is fabulous," she said.

Chapter 16

"Come away with me," Raoul pleaded. "It will only be for a week, I promise. Surely you can find that much time."

"As much as I enjoy being on the yacht and sailing, I just don't think I can be away right now. Please try to understand."

He was conscious of the fact she hadn't mentioned spending time with him. Anger flashed in Raoul's eyes. Even with Stephen's death, Raoul had not seen the changes in Tammy he had hoped for.

"Maybe you just don't want to spend time with me," he spouted.

"Now, Raoul," she soothed and lied, "you know that's not the case."

He mellowed a bit and continued his case.

"I know this little place off the coast of Europe. It's a tiny village where we can relax and enjoy ourselves for a few days. Get some sun. Indulge in some fine food."

Tammy was firm. Steeling herself against his persuasiveness, she continued softly, not willing to witness another outburst of his temper.

"Raoul, I really can't leave at this time. There's all this mess with the business and I don't trust Greg that much right now. You're a businessman. You know how important trust is. I have a lot of responsibility and I'm working to sort things out. I need to think clearly. Besides, my mother is here visiting and I don't think I should leave her here and run off to some secluded spot."

She saw the anger and hurt in his eyes.

"Just not right now, Raoul. Please be patient with me."

But he could no longer contain his emotion.

"Will you ever find a time for us, Tammy? I thought with Stephen gone..."

He saw her reaction to his words and stopped right there. It was best he left before he made things worse.

She stared after him as he slammed the door and for an instant thought perhaps she should go after him, but didn't. Something was always holding her back. Perhaps it was his temper she was afraid of. Or maybe it was his secretiveness about the rest of his life that made her uneasy. And why was Raoul still in her life? Was it because she enjoyed his lavish lifestyle? If she was truthful with herself, that hadn't really made her happy. Recently there had been times she had considered removing him from her life. But, even now, the thought of that sent chills through her at what he might possibly do under those circumstances. At any rate, right now she needed to concentrate on company business. Sometimes she wondered if by leaving his assets to her was some kind of punishment from Stephen. No. He would never do that. He trusted her to do the right thing even though they were divorced.

Raoul found his way to the street where a car was waiting for him. Immediately upon his arrival, three men in suits rushed to open doors and the car sped down the highway. Why was he so unhappy? He had money. He had fine things, possessions. He had power. But he didn't have the one thing he wanted...and that was Tammy Woods. And that irritated a man like Raoul.

"Radio ahead and have the yacht ready for sailing by afternoon," he commanded.

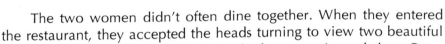

The two women didn't often dine together. When they entered the restaurant, they accepted the heads turning to view two beautiful women as a natural thing. Each had often experienced that. Once comfortably seated with dinner ordered, it was time for discussion.

"How are the business proceedings going with Greg Carter?" Margaret asked.

Tammy smiled.

"Right to the point, eh, mother?"

"Well, it's not like we chat every day, Tammy. Have to make up for lost time."

Giving a sigh as only her mother could provoke, Tammy launched into the details, finishing with her uneasiness.

"I just am not comfortable in the situation," she finally admitted.

"Then, listen to your heart," Margaret advised. "You've always had a strong sense of right and wrong and I am convinced Stephen knew what he was doing when he left this in your hands...your capable hands."

"Thanks, mother," Tammy said.

"Once you become a mother, you just can't turn a switch and forget all about being a mother. You should know that."

"You're right, of course."

Margaret's mind leaped back to the days spent at the villa during Candy's pregnancy when she tried to make those last few months as easy as she could for her granddaughter. Tears welled up in her eyes at the image of Candy's baby girl. So precious! So dear!

Finding another avenue of conversation seemed the best choice.

"Is Greg bothering you?"

Tammy considered her mother's question and the answer she was about to give.

"I don't think that's it at all although I confess I've played that scenario over in my mind."

"Remember, Tammy, Greg proposed to you once. And you turned him down for Stephen. It's very possible he has never gotten over that."

"That could be true, but I think he genuinely cared for Gina. I think he would have done anything for her."

Margaret was quick to take advantage of the opening.

"Even to the point of killing Stephen...or having him killed?" she asked.

Tammy was shocked.

"Mother! How could you? No, I don't think Greg could do something like that."

"Perhaps Stephen marrying not one, but two women Greg wanted would be motive enough."

Tammy was clearly upset by the tone of the conversation.

"Let's just change the subject," she suggested.

"Okay, what about Raoul? When are you going to remove him from your life? I know he does not make you happy, Tammy. I've always been concerned about his shady business deals and I've witnessed his angry outbursts of temper."

"Mother!"

"He hasn't threatened you, has he? Has he tried to hurt you?"

"Really, mother! Is my relationship Raoul and I have any business of yours?"

"This family is my business and I know you haven't always thought very clearly since you left Stephen. And I've seen how that has affected each one of the children. And, yes, their well-being is my concern as well. Gracious, Tammy, you've lost touch with your own children. You haven't been aware that Cliff has a gambling debt bigger than the state of Maryland. And Candy..."

"What about Candy?"

Margaret had already said too much.

"Well, you know how she's still searching to find herself, so to speak," she tried to cover up.

"Oh, here comes our soup. We'd better eat before it gets cold."

All during the dinner meal, Tammy digested the things her mother had said. True, she hadn't been aware of Cliff's gambling. Sadly, she realized most of what her mother said was true. She had been out of touch with the children and it was time she found a way back into their lives and to distance herself from Raoul. But just how was she to do that?

The sun shone brightly overhead as the 75 foot yacht cut through the blue green waters; and Raoul sat in a deck chair totally relaxed with a drink in his hand, sunglasses covering his eyes, his dark hair blowing in the breeze. A buxom blonde girl sat on one side of him and a raven-haired beauty on the other. He wasn't about to let Tammy Woods ruin a good time. If there was one strength he'd learned to cultivate, it was the one of putting people in positions he might later use to his advantage. Perhaps it was time he put some of those to use. If there were people who stood in his way of getting what he wanted, he would find some way of putting pressure on them or eliminating them altogether. It had always worked for him in the past. He had surrounded himself with men who were loyal to him. Whatever these men were to the rest of the world, they were devoted to him. And he paid them well. He could afford to. Those who proved unworthy suddenly came up missing.

But even the beauty of the ocean and the distraction of the girls didn't seem to help his anxiety today.

"Get me ship to shore," he demanded and was instantly brought the telephone.

Waving the girls aside, he placed the call.

"Yeah, he's hooked on gambling. I want him kept on the hook. Understand? I know his debt has been paid. You can bring him in again. Lure him with something...anything."

Raoul lit a cigar and settled back in his chair with a smile on his face. There was nothing he liked better than a good cigar...that and figuring out a way to control people.

Chapter 17

Tuesday mornings were pretty much all alike at Woods & Carter. But this particular Tuesday Katie arrived earlier than normal. She sat down at her desk, letting a sigh escape from her lips, feeling exhausted before the day even began. How long had this office been in turmoil? True, the staff continued to work each day, but since Stephen Woods' death…his murder…nothing had been the same and production as well as morale was at an all-time low. Emotions ran high enough with the first murder and then the surprise second death…that of Gina Woods…caused the upheaval to continue. And on top of that, the arrest of Zoe Carter, Mr. Carter's wife, for Gina's murder took everyone by surprise again. And now Tammy Woods was in the office almost every day making minor adjustments. And Mr. Carter was either secluded in his office or yelling at everyone. Appointments were kept waiting or not met at all. Frustration superseded any other emotion the staff felt. And the whispering and gossip never seemed to cease with new speculations rising every day. So it was no wonder Katie wanted to get to her desk to catch up on things before the executives, drama and other distractions were due to arrive.

She had been working for most of an hour, keeping careful watch on the clock. At five minutes 'til nine, the front doors opened and a group of fellow workers descended on the work place. Among them was Nash Adams carrying a small white bag.

"Morning," he said with a smile as he approached her desk. "Been here long?"

"About an hour," Katie answered, glancing at the clock. "I got my desk pretty well cleared. At least I can see the top of it now."

"Good for you…"

At that point the front doors opened once again and through them came Greg Carter with a bluster of confusion. His disheveled appearance…which had become the norm lately…attested to the torment he experienced and obviously was in another one of his foul moods.

"Oh, no," Katie breathed.

"What's going on here?" Mr. Carter slurred. "Isn't anyone working today? I should fire all of you!"

Flinging his arm to include the entire office staff with his message, he reeled a bit and it became clear that Greg Carter had been drinking.

"Hold on there," Nash said as he reached to steady the man.

Greg Carter pulled his arm from Nash's assistance.

"What are you doing? Who are you, anyway? Do I know you? Do you work here?" Greg questioned as he breathed heavily in Nash's face.

"Oh, I know," he continued, poking his finger into Nash's chest. "You're that nosy private detective, aren't you? Always snooping around asking questions. Well, I'm not answering questions today, so get out!"

He attempted to gesture towards the door to direct Nash's path, staggered and lost his balance. Katie covered her mouth with her hand in an attempt to contain the gasp that threatened to escape. At that point, Tammy Woods made her entrance. She quickly sized up the situation.

"Oh, for heaven's sake, Greg" she exclaimed, "What are you doing? My goodness, you're drunk! Come on. You're making a spectacle of yourself."

At the sound of Tammy's voice, he became child-like and began to cry.

"Oh, Tammy, you've always been good to me," he blubbered. "Always been good for me. Why didn't we ever get together? He didn't deserve you."

With that he sobbed loudly as the entire office watched the drama unfold.

But Tammy had taken control of the situation; and reaching for his arm, she coaxed him into following her under the gaze of stunned office employees.

"Maybe because you do dumb things, Greg. Let's get you into your office. Clarice, could you please bring in some coffee? And make it strong and black. Everyone, please continue with your work. Mr. Carter simply isn't himself these days."

With that declaration, she steered Greg towards his office door while the office slowly resumed its usual hum of gossip and work.

"Well, that was interesting," Nash said as he turned towards Katie who stood wide-eyed, not knowing for sure if she could hold back the tears.

"It's been that way for days," she said. "I think he's having an emotional break down."

"And if he doesn't, some of the rest of us just might," she added.

Nash took her hand in his.

"I'm here," he said. "Let me help you."

"What do you think you can do?" she said and the tears began to flow freely.

"Well, for starters, I can treat you to this doughnut I brought for you. Let me get a couple of cups of coffee and let's go in to that little break room and sit for a few minutes."

She followed him, perfectly willing to let him take care of her, grateful for his presence. Within a few minutes, Nash's words had calmed her and she was smiling.

"Thanks, Nash. I needed you today."

"Anytime. You okay now?" he asked.

"Yes. I think I'll be okay now and can get back to work. I don't know what came over me. I'm not usually given to tears."

The notes had come steadily since she returned from Europe without the baby. As if leaving her baby girl hadn't been traumatic enough, then came the notes. Each month they arrived. And she never knew when they would arrive; she just knew they would come. Sometimes left in her car, never by mail. They might appear under a napkin at a restaurant or hand delivered by someone who immediately disappeared into the crowd of students as she entered a classroom at school. Never signed, just a reminder that someone out there knew about the baby. Whoever it was never asked for money. Someone just wanted her to know they knew her secret. Apparently it was information to be stored away until such time it could be used advantageously for the person responsible for sending the reminders.

But it wore on Candy's emotions to think someone was out there anticipating her every move. And what could the police do? There was no intent in the notes although she had kept them all hidden away in a box in the top of her closet. There was no real threat, just a subtle reminder. And the burden was a heavy one. She frequently found herself looking over her shoulder to see if she was being followed and quite often she had that sensation. However, no one ever approached her.

Perspiration broke out on Cliff's forehead and his breath came in short gasps. Had he dreamed it? No, he definitely had been approached with an offer he could not refuse. Money extended to him to use for gambling. He'd been welcomed back, even escorted to the eleventh floor of The Gateway, given free drinks and perks. And he'd won! Won big! The rush of adrenalin he felt was unbelievable. He was back and he was back on top.

Not once did the image of Grandma Hastings bailing him out of the gambling debt enter his mind. Other people lost at gambling. He couldn't lose. Gambling was something he was good at. A winning streak had begun and Cliff's pulse quickened at the thought. He couldn't wait to get back to the tables.

"Nash, my boy, we haven't seen you around much," Mr. Meijer said as Nash made his way through the small delicatessen at the end of the day. "Kinda late for you, isn't it?"

Mr. Meijer was just cleaning up and had put the closed sign in the front window of the delicatessen before he lowered the window shades.

"I've been busy so thought I'd come in and do some work I've gotten behind on," Nash replied. "How've you been?"

"Oh, good, good. Business is good. We have a new sandwich on the menu now."

"That's really great," Nash was genuinely happy to see Mr. Meijer's enthusiasm.

There was something comforting about the atmosphere the Meijer family created in their little delicatessen and it was something that kept regular customers coming back and hopefully information they would share with their friends...Meijer's delicatessen had great food. Nash always felt right at home there. He realized he'd been too busy lately and had missed the company of the Meijer family.

"Oh, by the way, you have a new neighbor," Mr. Meijer said as he gestured towards the second floor.

"I never got acquainted with the other tenants."

"They didn't stay long. These people paid ahead of time...and in cash."

"What's their business?" Nash inquired.

"I don't really know," Mr. Meijer was quick to add, "but they paid ahead of time...and in cash."

Nash smiled.

"I'll look forward to meeting them. I'll try to do that before they move out."

He smiled again and wondered if Mr. Meijer understood the humor in his statement.

"Anne at home?" he asked.

"Oh, yes. Anne's a good girl and she is a big help now that school is out."

"I know. I've appreciated her help with this case I'm working on."

"Yah, that's all she talks about. I'm sure if she knows you're here, she'll want to bother you."

"No bother," Nash said as he headed for the stairs. "Send her on up."

Fifteen minutes later, Anne appeared at his office door.

"Papa says I shouldn't be a bother."

"Nonsense. Come on in. I enjoy your company."

Nash and Anne went over the photos on the wall and discussed some of the new developments of the case. Nash felt comfortable sharing the details with Anne but cautioned her that confidentiality was an important part of being a private investigator. She was a good listener and sometimes when he verbalized his thoughts, things became clearer to him as well.

She shared the second part of her paper she was writing on the world of a private investigator and made it clear there was no specific mention of the current case. Once again, she had the enthusiasm he'd witnessed before when she was sharing with him and he was impressed with her thoroughness. Anne really was quite good at what she did.

"Have you met the new tenants?" Nash wanted to know.

"Not officially. I saw two of them and told Papa I was concerned. But he just said they had paid ahead…and paid in cash."

Nash smiled at the repeating of the phrase he'd heard earlier from Mr. Meijer.

"Why would you have reason to be concerned?"

"I'm not sure. Just a feeling I had when I saw the two men dressed in black. Only had briefcases with them. Nothing else. They just seemed sort of creepy to me. I kinda got a chill when I saw them."

"Hmm," Nash's thoughts were whirling inside his head.

He never underestimated gut feelings. He had trusted his own on many occasions and found them to be fairly accurate. After Anne left and he had completed his work and as Nash left the office, he saw a light shining under the door to the room next to his. Since the hour was late, he chose to refrain from knocking on the door. Double checking the lock on the door to his own office, Nash walked down the stairs, made his way through the deli and into the night.

He hadn't gone far when he got the feeling he wasn't alone. Reaching for his gun, he was secure that it was in a resting position against his skin; and trying to ignore the sensation creeping up his neck, he chose to walk in the opposite direction from his parked car, being careful to stay close to the street lamps. When crossing the street and checking the traffic, he took the opportunity to scan the street for any activity. All was quiet except for a slight motion of what he believed to be a man ducking into the doorway of an all-night drugstore. He took the opportunity to run to the seclusion of an alleyway, emerging into the light of the next street, doubled back, found his car and sped towards home.

Chapter 18

"We have eyes on him."

"Good. Be discreet. I don't want him hurt, just scared a bit."

"Okay, boss."

"You had any trouble in renting the space?"

"None. Meijer was glad to get the cash in his hands."

"Good. And keep me posted. I don't want any surprises, understand?"

"You got it, boss."

The caller put his cell phone back in his pocket, exited the convenience store and entered the dark street.

"Where'd he go?"

"Ran and ducked down the alley," the second man answered.

"You think he saw us?"

"Probably. That's why he ran."

"No problem," said the first. "We'll pick him up again tomorrow."

"Good. I'm hungry. Let's go find something to eat."

The two men dressed in black made their way down the street.

"You checked in with the boss?"

"Yeah."

Greg Carter's car sped into the night. He had no particular destination. He just wanted to get past the agony that consumed his mind. Plans for the future had been so clear just a few short weeks ago. Now he was grasping at straws; and he was well aware such mentality could be a fatal mistake for him. He suffered from insomnia and the alcohol he consumed every day did not seem to help block out the facts.

And the company was suffering from his inability to make decisions. Maybe if he hadn't argued with Stephen and things hadn't gotten out of hand. At times he thought he was losing his mind. If it weren't for Tammy...dear Tammy, Tammy who had always had a special place in his heart. But she had chosen Stephen all those years ago and it had eaten at him ever since. Stephen didn't deserve her. Never did. A lifetime of bitterness welled up inside him.

A blast from a car horn as a car sped by him jarred his thoughts. He struggled to concentrate on keeping his car in the proper lane. Up ahead he saw the lights of a bar he frequented. As he wheeled into the parking lot, his mouth began to anticipate the alcohol. Soon he would be feeling better...or not feeling anything at all. And that was okay. He needed to forget and soothe his conscience.

"I know this quaint little shop," Candy was telling Grandmother Hastings. "My friends and I found it and I really like the merchandise they carry in their store. You want to go check it out?"

"Sure," Margaret Hastings answered. "I'm always interested in new places."

That was a quality in Grandmother Hastings Candy admired.

It was an outing for grandmother and granddaughter, something that hadn't happened since their time spent together in Europe and that had been limited by the last days of Candy's pregnancy and the arrival of little Stephanie. And Candy's trips since that time had been spent with baby Stephanie.

Grandma Hastings found the shop just as delightful as Candy and friends had and she was particularly impressed with the salesgirl. The shop was busy with shoppers coming in and out, making purchases, but it still came as a surprise.

As Candy placed the clothes for purchase on the counter, she saw the envelope. Instantly she knew what it was. Grabbing it, she attempted to conceal it, but Grandma Hastings was too quick to notice.

"What's that?" she questioned.

"Oh, nothing," Candy responded as she pushed it into her bag.

Grandma Hastings did not pursue the questioning...at least not until they sat across from each other at lunch.

"When are you planning another trip to Europe?" Margaret Hastings asked.

Candy sighed as she slumped back in her chair.

"These past few weeks have been so crazy," she began. "I miss Dad so much! And being without Stephanie is torture."

With that remark, tears instantly filled her eyes and Grandmother Hastings reached over and put a consoling hand on Candy's hand.

"We women can be a whole lot stronger than people give us credit for," she attempted to reassure. "Sweetie, you've been through a lot in a short amount of time. Step back and take a deep breath."

Her comment was followed by a short pause.

"But, I understand. I'm a mother, too, you know," she continued in a different tone, "Stephanie is such a beautiful child and she's being well taken care of. I visited with her right before I caught the flight here. She's starting to walk now. And your father would have been happy with the name choice."

Candy immediately burst into tears.

"Oh, I'm sorry," Grandmother apologized. "I shouldn't have brought that up."

"It's not only that," Candy sobbed.

Margaret Hastings moved to a chair closer to her granddaughter. Putting her arm around her, she continued.

"What is it, dear? Does this have something to do with that envelope at the clothing store?"

Maybe it was time to share the burden and who better to share it with than Grandmother Hastings? Grandmother had already shared her deepest joys and sorrows. Reaching inside her purse, Candy placed the envelope in Grandmother Hastings' hands. Grandmother Hastings took the envelope and looked at Candy.

"Go ahead," Candy encouraged. "Go ahead and open it."

Grandmother Hastings opened the envelope; and removing the piece of paper inside, she quickly scanned the message.

"Oh, my goodness," she exclaimed. "What is this all about? Is this what I think it is? Well, of course it is. Blackmail, plain and simple. Do they want money?"

Candy shook her head.

"Not yet."

"There are some things money can't solve."

"There are others...other letters. I have a whole shoebox full of them."

"Who...?"

"I don't know. All I know is that they just appear and someone knows about my baby...my Stephanie."

Again the tears flowed.

"May I keep this?"

"Why not?"

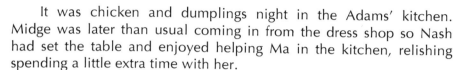

It was chicken and dumplings night in the Adams' kitchen. Midge was later than usual coming in from the dress shop so Nash had set the table and enjoyed helping Ma in the kitchen, relishing spending a little extra time with her.

`"Any progress on your murder case?" Ma asked.

"Things keep happening and new facts come to light, but still nothing strong enough to make an arrest," he informed.

Ma patted Nash on the back.

"It will. Patience," she said.

"Yeah, I know. Not the easiest thing... this waiting."

Ma lifted the lid on the pan to check the progress of the dumplings.

"Um, just about done. I hope Midge will be here soon," she commented.

Tony chose that time to make his entrance. Since school had been out for the summer, he had found a job at the local garage where he was learning a few things about mechanics and hard work. That was good. Time to learn that money quite frequently is accompanied by diligent work.

"Hey, brother," he commented. "Solved any murders lately?"

"Not yet," Nash replied as he placed the salad bowl on the table.

"But he will soon," Ma chimed in, being the ever positive mother.

Midge chose that moment to come in the back door; and kicking off her shoes, she uttered a sigh as she reached for a glass of cold water.

"Long day?" Nash asked.

"Endless. And my feet are living proof."

"Well, you two get washed up," Ma directed. "Supper is ready."

As usual, the conversation at Ma's table was both informative and supportive.

"Nash," Ma said as she placed a good-sized helping of dumplings on Tony's plate, "you need to speak with Tony. He thinks he could get a better job."

Nash looked at his little brother.

"Is that right?"

"Yeah, I'm tired of this job. I think I could do better and make more money someplace else."

"Umm."

Tony knew there was more to come from his big brother.

"You have the assurance of another job?"

"Not exactly."

"I'll take that as a no."

Silence.

"Umm."

"Umm, what?" Tony asked impatiently.

"Oh, I don't know. I've always known Mr. Crankston to be a fair man. And I'm sure you're learning a lot while you're there."

It was half question, half statement.

"Yeah, but I don't have any free time. And the guys want to go up to the lake next week and I want to go, too. I could give my notice and then I'd be free to go."

Nash was slow to speak, knowing it gave him time to think and it let words sink into Tony's sometimes stubborn brain.

"That's true. But what if you can't get another job? Then you have no money to do anything anyway."

Tony frowned at that thought.

"What if you continue to work through the rest of the summer and maybe take off the last week before school starts? Then you will have the satisfaction of having been successfully employed for the summer, have a little money and a little break before school starts again. Maybe you can plan something with your friends then."

No response. Tony's head dropped with disappointment.

"Does that sound reasonable?" Nash asked after a reasonable length of time.

"I guess," Tony answered although it didn't sound as if he was completely sold on the idea.

The meal continued in silence for a few minutes with only the sound of silverware clinking against glass.

"Candy was in the store today," Midge said. "With an older...very stylish...older woman."

"Her grandmother," Nash explained. "And? There's more?"

"Well, a strange thing happened. When I was folding the clothes and checking them out, there was this envelope under them. Just kind of appeared out of nowhere. And it had Candy's name on the outside. She grabbed it like she didn't want anyone to see it and stuck it in her purse."

"Umm. That is strange. I'll tuck that piece of information away for future reference," Nash concluded.

Wiping his mouth with a napkin, Nash redirected the conversation.

"Great chicken and dumplings, Ma."

There was a consensus of agreement at the table.

"Oh, I do have a bit of news," Nash began. "I seem to have new neighbors in the room next to me above the delicatessen."

"Really?" Midge commented. "Have you met them yet?"

"Not yet. Anne Meijer says she saw them and is a bit suspicious of them. Says they moved in with nothing but a couple of briefcases."

"Well, once you meet them, you can form an opinion for yourself," Ma suggested.

"Of course. But Anne does have a sixth sense about her. I've learned to value her opinion."

"Okay, okay," Tony blurted out. "I'll keep the job...but you gotta remember...you promised I could take that last week off."

"Sounds like a smart decision to me," Nash replied, smiling to himself that Tony had been mulling things over in his own mind while the others conversed.

"That's the same advice your Pop would have given you," Ma said to Tony as she nodded in approval at her older son's advice and her younger son's decision.

"Hurry up, Stokes. We ain't got all day to get this done. The kid will likely be here soon."

"I'm hurryin' as fast as I can," came the second voice.

"I think I hear someone comin'," the first man said.

"There. It's done," Stokes said. "Now we should be able to hear anything that goes on next door."

The first man carefully opened the door to the room ever so slightly.

"Is it him?" Stokes asked.

"Naw, it's some older broad," came the reply.

"That's good. If this works, we ought to have something to report to the boss by evening."

Nash bounded up the stairs from Meijer's delicatessen to his second floor office only to be met by Margaret Shore Hastings waiting at his door.

"Well, good morning," he greeted.

Margaret Shore Hastings glanced at her watch, reminding Nash he was five minutes late according to the hours written on the office door.

"What brings you here this early in the morning?" he asked as he fumbled for his keys.

Margaret scanned the hallway and nodded towards the door.

"We'll talk inside," she said.

Once inside, she whispered to him.

"I have reason to believe we are being watched," she began. "At least someone is watching my granddaughter."

"Perhaps you should start at the beginning," Nash suggested. "Have a seat. You look upset."

"Yes," Margaret said as she sat down in the chair offered. "And I don't upset very easily as you may have figured out."

"Here, would you like some water?" Nash asked.

"Thanks," she said as she twisted the cap and took a long drink.

Nash settled himself behind the old desk.

"Now, what's this all about?"

Margaret took another drink of water and then opened her purse.

"My granddaughter has been receiving these notes, these threats. No, I guess they're not really threats. It's just that someone out there knows things about her that they shouldn't know."

"Whoa, here. Hold up a bit," Nash interrupted. "Which granddaughter are we talking about?"

"Oh, I guess I am rattled. Candy. My granddaughter, Candy."

"Okay, Candy. Now who is behind these?"

"We don't know."

"What kinds of things do these notes imply?"

"Here. Here, read for yourself. This is just the latest one. She says there are a whole box of them that she's saved.

Nash took the envelope; and taking the note from it, he read.

"Are they all this vague?" he asked.

"That's what she says. Never asks for money or anything like that. Just a gentle reminder. And delivered at various times and places. Like today...no one knew we were going to that little dress shop."

Nash remembered Midge's account from the previous evening.

"This fits in with the information we spoke of the other evening. Go over the facts again with me."

Margaret Hastings settled back in the chair and began the story.

"Candy came to me...in Europe...about a year and a half ago. She was pregnant and was quite sure the young man involved would not be a welcome addition to the family. Didn't want her parents to know so she chose to hide the fact, but she wanted to keep the baby. Anyway, she came to me under the guise of spending time abroad. She had the baby...a girl...and a couple I knew of are caring for the child. It broke Candy's heart to have to leave her, but the couple welcomes her anytime she can come to visit. No one has ever known...up 'til now."

"So this person could be someone who was in Europe at the time of the birth and somehow found out or someone who ran across the information here in the states," Nash summed up. "Do you have any suspicions? How about someone at the hospital?"

"It's a very small town, Nash. I would trust anyone who lives there. Besides, we were very careful."

Margaret thought for a moment.

"Nash, if it's a matter of money...you know I have plenty. If that would help. And your fee, too," she added.

The photos on the wall of the office continued to draw Margaret's attention.

"Do you see a likely suspect?" Nash asked, noticing her interest.

"Only two," she replied.

"Hello."

"Hey, boss, this is Stokes. It's working. The kid knows about the notes."

Chapter 19

Hanging out at the precinct was a favorite pastime for Nash. He learned a lot being around the hustle and bustle of the detectives and of course it was always good to share the latest developments in the case with his good buddy, Louie.

"You got any gut feelings about this Woods case?" he asked over a cup of coffee.

"Can't say that I do. Interesting development with the note business. I tried to lift some fingerprints from it, but that was near to impossible. There's been no word on anything new from the police department in Colorado either?"

Nash shook his head and thought a few moments before he spoke.

"The only clue I have is the peculiar behavior of Greg Carter. He certainly appears to be going off the deep end. Whether it's from guilt or losing Gina or his wife being a murderer is hard to tell. I know one thing for sure...things aren't going well at the offices of Woods & Carter."

"How so?"

"Business is taking a nose dive. He just seems to not be able to concentrate. Why, the other day when I was there, he came in drunk at nine in the morning."

Louie seemed to be processing that.

"You still seeing that girl from there?"

"Yeah. She's easy to be with. Hey, maybe she's got a friend," Nash teased.

Nash and Louie had been on a lot of double dates throughout their high school years, some of which turned out really badly but made for some good laughs now."

"No, thanks. I'm sure she's a really nice girl, but I've had some experience with girls who are friends of the girls you date. I may be a slow learner, but eventually I get it."

They both laughed at the memories.

———————◆●◆———————

Tammy Carter hit the alarm, pulled the covers over her head and rolled over in bed. Not today, she thought. Today is my day!

But as much as she wanted it to be her day, she could not go back to sleep so she stumbled to the small kitchen of the apartments at The Gateway for a cup of coffee. She preferred not to stay at the house, the one she and Stephen had shared. The apartment was okay as far as apartments go...temporarily...but she missed her house in the suburbs of Detroit. The fact was, she needed to be involved in the company so the apartment would have to do. With Greg's bizarre behavior, it only made good business sense for her to stick around and be knowledgeable. Is this what Stephen had in mind when he left it all to her in his will? Sometimes she found herself resenting that fact. Other times she felt proud he thought her capable enough to figure it out.

Plus, being in town afforded her the opportunity to be closer to the children...and away from Raoul. And her mother was right. She hardly knew her own children any more. The distance between them had widened in the last two years. After the divorce. Was it her fault? Or was it just the natural evolvement of life?

Taking a piece of toast from the toaster and spreading it with butter and jelly, she sat at the table with her cup of coffee. Well, although she was awake, she still didn't have to plunge into the day. This was the kind of day to put on some smooth music, take a long, hot bath, read a good book or all of the above. No, she wouldn't even leave the apartment. She'd just spend a quiet day alone and restore her spirit. Good heavens, she certainly deserved that much. Being a business woman was exhausting, especially under the circumstances.

Bath water was running and she found herself humming a tune that somehow had remained in her head and wouldn't leave while she studied her face in the mirror when the phone rang.

"Tammy, this is your mother. I'm coming over."

Tammy's answer wasn't quick enough and the line went dead. It wouldn't have made any difference anyway, she thought. Once Margaret Shore Hastings made up her mind to do something, no one, including her daughter, was about to change it. Tammy turned off the water; and wrapping her robe around her, made her way to the apartment door.

Margaret Shore Hastings breezed through it as soon as it was opened.

That was just one advantage to having apartments in the same building.

"Why don't you come in, mother?" Tammy said sarcastically.

"Why aren't you dressed?" Margaret continued. "No wonder this younger generation never gets anything done. No early start to the day."

"Hello, mother," the sarcasm continued. "Good to see you, too."

Margaret seemed to be taking in every inch of the apartment as she talked.

"Oh, yes, good morning. Is that coffee I smell?"

"It is," Tammy said as she closed the door. "Would you like a cup?"

"Well, sure, but I can't stay. I just dropped by to invite you to dinner tonight. Lindy's coming back in town and we're all getting together this evening."

How could her mother be more in touch with her children than she was? When did this happen? Tammy fumbled with the coffee.

"Have a seat," she said as she took some cookies from a container and placed them on a plate in front of her mother.

"Umm, home-baked," Margaret said as she sampled one of them. "You always were a good cook. I never cared much for it myself."

"I know."

Just then Tammy's cell phone went off.

"Raoul. Are you still on the yacht?" Tammy asked, completely ignoring the roll of Margaret's eyes and the sigh of exasperation that escaped her lips.

"In the harbor? No. No, I can't. I have plans for tonight."

Margaret was imagining the side of the conversation she could not hear.

"No. It's with family if you must know. Lindy's back in town so the children and I...and my mother...are getting together for dinner."

"No, I don't know where at this point. Mother just dropped by to tell me the plans. She's here right now."

147

Tammy didn't really want to deal with Raoul's temperament at this moment.

"I have to go now. Good-bye."

And Tammy laid the phone on the table.

"Don't say it, mother," she warned.

"I don't need to," Margaret replied. "You already know how I feel. I don't trust him. I wish he wasn't in your life. I think he is trouble. Name one good thing about that man."

"He's..." she faltered.

"See, that's my point. You can't say he's thoughtful or caring or protective or..."

"Okay, mother, I get your point."

"And, Tammy, I know that you may never get over Stephen."

"Well," Tammy snapped. "There you have it. That's one thing you and Raoul have in common. Neither one of you thinks I've gotten over Stephen. Well, maybe I haven't and maybe I never will."

"Filling your life with something worthwhile would help," Margaret retaliated.

"I know how you feel, mother."

"Good. Now that we have that settled, I'll be going. I'll see you tonight at dinner. At the Escape at 7 sharp."

The cell phone went off again. Tammy looked at it and chose to ignore it. If Raoul was on another tirade, she was in no mood to deal with him.

With that Margaret Shore Hastings made her exit and Tammy curled up in the oversized chair near the window. Her mother was right about Raoul. Tammy just didn't want to hear it. Raoul was controlling and possessive and at times, sinister. Still, Tammy felt something that closely resembled fear when she thought about what he could do or might do if she told him she didn't want to see him anymore. She'd felt the effects of his bad temper. There had been the time he'd left bruises on her arm when he grabbed her. And once he had doubled his fist and she thought he might strike her, but he hadn't. Lately, she'd been hoping he would find someone else who appealed to him and perhaps that would get him out of her life.

Just now, Tammy seemed to think the best solution was the plate of cookies. She reached for them; and one by one, she proceeded to devour them.

The cell phone sailed across the deck of the yacht.
"Get me a drink," he demanded.
People began scurrying to meet his needs.
"And get the boys on the phone. I've got a job for them to do."

Lindy stepped down from the plane and made her way to the baggage claim carousels. Jetting around the world and spending time with her friends had not taken away the ache she felt for the loss of her father so she was making her way back to family. Dressed in jeans and a yellow crop top, her blue eyes hidden behind sunglasses, she concentrated on identifying her luggage and failed to notice the two men dressed in black who watched her every move.

She hadn't let anyone know she was coming in on this early flight so she wouldn't be expected until later in the day. Finding her suitcases, she called for a cab and waited at the curb for it to arrive. The airport was busy and people were bustling about her, pushing and hurrying. A man bumped into her and she startled.

"Sorry, ma'am," he said as he pulled his hat down over his face and kept going.

A screaming toddler distracted her.

Lindy tugged at the strap of her bag slung over her shoulder and pulled her luggage closer to her. Luckily the champagne colored SUV pulled up in good time; and the driver, dressed in black, hopped out to load her luggage.

"Miss Woods?" he mumbled.

"Yes," she answered as she made herself comfortable in the back seat as the driver began to dodge in and out of the heavy airport traffic.

Chapter 20

"She should be here by now," Grandmother Hastings fussed. "It's not like Lindy to be late."

"Well, she's not the most responsible person," Susan snapped.

"Oh, Susan," Cliff chastised, "just because everyone isn't quite as punctual and perfect as you are doesn't mean they're not responsible."

Susan rolled her eyes.

"Whatever!"

"Here comes mother," Candy said when she saw her mother turn heads as she made her entrance through the restaurant doors, clad in a summery pink blouse and print skirt and straw sandals.

Tammy greeted each one of her children with a hug and a kiss.

"Where's Lindy?" she asked as she looked around.

"That was just the topic of conversation," Margaret took it upon herself to explain.

"That's not like Lindy," Tammy observed.

"Exactly what I said," Grandmother Hastings agreed.

None of the children missed the roll of their mother's eyes.

"Maybe someone should call," Grandmother Hastings continued.

Immediately four cell phones were in the hands of their owners and buttons were being put to good use. All listened carefully to the number of rings and then the message and each one left an urgent plea to be answered.

Lindy watched out the window as she rode in the back of the vehicle. Her cell phone lay in her lap although she still didn't feel the need to let anyone know she was in town. Taking a deep breath, she felt a calm just thinking about being with family again. No one should be home and they weren't expecting her until evening so she had the entire day to relax in her old room at the house on Hickory Lane. Maybe she'd even go for a swim in the pool on such a glorious day. As she watched the scenery through the car window, it became increasingly apparent to her that this was not the way to the house on Hickory Lane.

"Excuse me," she said as she tapped on the window separating passenger from driver. "Can you hear me? I believe this is not the way to the address I gave you."

There was no response and she tapped on the window once again and then frantically began to pound on it with her fist. The cell phone fell to the floor as she desperately tried to get the attention of the driver. No response. She stared in horror at the back of his head. Everything about this spelled out danger. Still the driver continued silently and then quite suddenly pulled into a deserted gas station. Thinking this seemed the perfect opportunity to escape, Lindy grabbed for the door handle but found it to be locked. Seconds later the door was opened and a strong hand grasped her arm and pulled her from the back seat. She screamed but the streets were deserted and there was no one to hear her. The man did not speak as he threw her suitcase out of the trunk and then returned to the car and sped away.

She watched as the car left and tried to read the license plate. She could only see the last three numbers. 5-8-6. Or were they 6-8-5? They seemed to blur in her memory. Lindy looked around for any source of help. None was available. She reached for her cell phone and then remembered it had fallen to the floor of the vehicle when she was trying to get to the driver. Guessing at which direction she would choose to walk, she shouldered her bag; and picking up the handle to the suitcase, she began the walk to find help.

She walked for several minutes before any traffic passed by. When cars did began to appear, apparently no one thought it strange to see a young blonde woman walking down a highway pulling her luggage behind her. It ought to raise some eyebrows, particularly since this was not a travel area like a bus station or airport where such a sight might not be unusual. A silver colored sedan pulled up beside her and the rear passenger window rolled down.

"Lindy, is that you?" Raoul asked.

She turned. What were the chances the man who knew her mother would be driving by at the exact time she needed someone? She was stunned.

Raoul opened the car door and hurried to her, putting his arms around her.

"What's wrong, Lindy? You look to be upset. Well, of course you are or you wouldn't be walking out here in the middle of nowhere. What has happened?"

She could not reply.

Raoul nodded towards his driver who was standing near the car and the driver put Lindy's suitcase in the back of the car while Raoul helped Lindy into the back seat.

Raoul patted Lindy's hand.

"Can you talk about it?" he asked.

He listened while she told him of the abduction as he attempted to comfort her. Then came the tears.

"Oh, my! What time is it?" Lindy gasped, looking at her watch. "I was supposed to meet the family at The Escape a half hour ago."

"Don't worry," Raoul said. "Dry your tears. We'll get you there. Stokes, take us to The Escape."

So it happened that Raoul walked Lindy Woods into the restaurant, hoping he would appear as the great rescuer to a very grateful Tammy Woods.

Lindy was in Nash's office the following morning. He listened carefully to the details of her abduction and rescue. Something about it didn't seem quite right.

"You realize that this is someone who knew when your plane would land, right?" he asked.

She hadn't thought about that facet of the situation.

"You're right," she stammered. "But who?"

"Who knew you were coming?"

"Just Grandma Hastings, I think," she confided. "She sent me a text saying the family would get together at the restaurant so I assume Mom and Cliff and Susan and Candy were all aware that I was coming in, but I specifically did not tell them which flight because I wanted to be in town for a while before I went to meet them at the restaurant."

Nash frowned.

"It would appear that whoever did this knew you were coming in sometime yesterday and took the trouble to check passenger flights. You say you got some numbers from the license plate?"

"Well, yes," she answered. "I think it was 5-8-6."

"But it could have been 6-8-5. I'm a little foggy on that. I was really scared."

"That's understandable," Nash consoled. "Do you know color or make or model?"

"No. Just that it was a light color."

The movement of the chair as Nash stood made a scraping sound and the man with the headphones in the next room grabbed at his ear.

"I'll take you down to the precinct and we'll see if that's enough information for Louie to run some numbers for us."

Neither Nash nor Lindy noticed the black SUV parked near the corner as they left the building.

Louie was glad to see them and put the numbers in the system without much success.

"Try running them against specific names," Nash suggested.

"Okay," Louie agreed, "but the chances of anyone using their own vehicle is pretty slim."

One match did come up. The numbers 5-8-6 were a part of the license plate on Zoe Carter's car.

"Doesn't make sense," Nash told Louie. "She said there was a window between the front and back seats. Ordinary cars don't come equipped with those."

"Hmm. You're right about that," Louie agreed. "But it's still information we might use later."

The door of Greg Carter's office flew open. It was as if that motion caused the entire office staff to freeze.

"I need someone in here," Greg demanded.

Turning in response to the blank stares that request received, he turned again before he slammed the office door.

"Now!"

Tammy Woods was not scheduled to be in the office at all this particular day. Several of the secretaries looked at each other in dismay. Finally one spoke.

"I'll go," Katie said as she straightened her shoulders for the task and walked slowly towards the door. Turning the handle, she announced her arrival and closed the door behind her, keeping her hands securely around the door handle.

"I'm here, Mr. Carter. What can I do for you?"

He sat motionless, his back to her, his chair facing the window. It was as if he was not aware of her presence. She took a step closer. Clearing her throat, thinking perhaps he hadn't heard her, she spoke again.

"Mr. Carter, you requested someone?"

"Maybe," his voice was low and strange sounding.

Then more silence.

"You asked for someone to come in, sir, so I came in response to your request."

The chair flew around so fast that Katie stepped back in surprise and once again gripped the door handle. Mr. Carter's face was red and contorted like nothing she'd ever seen. Mr. Carter had always been immaculate in his appearance, neat and clean shaven. The man who sat before her portrayed an entirely different image. It appeared he had slept in his clothes, if indeed he had slept at all. His eyes were red and blurry as if he had been crying and there was the look of a wild and tormented man in them. His usually crisp white shirt was stained and unbuttoned at the top, allowing his tie to droop down the front of it. She guessed his hair had been neither washed nor combed in some time.

"What are you staring at?" he slurred. "Who are you anyway?"

Katie tried to remain calm.

"I'm Katie," she said, trying hard to keep her voice from shaking. "I'm here to help you."

Her words seem to soothe him. But once again she was shocked when Mr. Carter began to sob uncontrollably.

"What is it, sir? How can I help you?"

"I've done a terrible thing, Katie," he uttered between sobs. "A terrible, terrible thing."

Nash had just left the precinct when he got her call. Katie sounded nervous on the phone when she'd called him from the offices of Woods & Carter.

"What's going on?"

"You'd better get over here right away," she said in a voice he'd never heard before.

"Katie, are you okay?" he asked.

"Yes, but please hurry."

He dodged through the heavy lunchtime traffic and raced through the doors of the Nelson Corporation, into the elevator where he impatiently waited its ascent. Maybe he could have made better time using the stairs. The fact that Katie needed him and the anxiousness in her voice continued to echo in his ears. A frantic Katie met him at the doors of Woods & Carter.

"What's going on?" he said as he attempted to gain his breath. "You look upset."

She collapsed in his arms and he held her for a few moments.

"It's Mr. Carter," she said, attempting to dry the tears that had now spilled out in relief upon seeing him. "I think he's having a nervous breakdown."

Nash looked past her into the office area. Tammy Woods had been called in as well as an emergency crew. Greg Carter was on his way to the hospital. They watched along with the rest of the staff of Woods & Carter, all in a state of confusion and dismay over the conduct of their once very capable leader. Slowly the office began to buzz about all they'd seen and heard and gathered around Katie, some complimenting her on her bravery and some asking for details.

Tammy Woods was there now lending some sort of stability to the situation with her quiet manner and skillful management of people until once again the area seemed more like a functioning office than a scene of havoc.

"Everyone needs to get back to work," she said. "Finish what you can and then take the afternoon off. I'm closing the office for the rest of the day. Work will resume promptly in the morning. If you need me, I'll be at the hospital."

Nash hurried Katie to the work room where he attempted to calm her. She was still shaking from the ordeal.

"I've never seen anyone like that. He's either a mad man or sobbing with remorse," she explained.

"Tell me everything from the beginning," Nash said calmly.

Calm was what Katie needed right now. Taking a deep breath, she organized her thoughts and methodically told him all she knew.

"But, Nash, he said he'd done a terrible thing," she confided. "Do you think...could he have...?"

Nash took her in his arms.

"I don't know, Katie. I don't know. But it sure seems like the evidence is pointing that direction."

Chapter 21

It was late afternoon before the doctors were able to examine Greg and come up with a diagnoses and treatment. Tammy Woods sat quietly in the waiting room. She'd conducted all the business she could via her phone and had resorted to thumbing through the outdated and tattered magazines wondering all the time about the number of germs she was probably picking up from them. Finally she was interrupted by a man in a white coat approaching her with news.

"Mrs. Woods?" he inquired, extending his hand. "You're here in behalf of Mr. Carter?"

"Yes, doctor, I am," she answered as she stood to greet him.

It was at that point Tammy realized that Greg was indeed alone. Zoe had gone to prison and they had never had any children. She pondered that for a time.

Doctor Bennett gestured towards the seats and they both moved to sit down.

"This is not a crucial situation...I mean, I believe it's fixable," he said. "He seems to be overworked, under extreme pressure...stress. I've prescribed some medication which should relax him and he'll be going off to sleep shortly. We'll keep him a couple of days for observation and perhaps I'll recommend some therapy. There's a really good doctor on staff here who deals with this kind of situation. I understand Mr. Carter has reason to be stressed."

"Yes...his wife and also his business partner."

Dr. Bennett shook his head. He listened to the local news.

"Thank you, doctor," Tammy said as she once again shook his hand.

"You can go in and see him now if you like...but just for a few minutes. He needs to remain quiet. Complete rest will make a big difference. You'll see."

He patted Tammy on the hand as a sign of reassurance and then left to assist others in need of his expertise.

Tammy gathered her things. The least she could do would be to visit with Greg to see for herself how things were with him before she left. Then she was ready to head back to the apartment to crash. All the emotion of last night and today had taken its toll on her as well.

"How's he doing?" Nash asked as he made his way down the corridor.

"Oh, hello, Nash," Tammy answered, not really all that surprised to see him.

"The doctor says he'll be alright. Just needs some rest. He's given him something to help him sleep. I was just on my way in there to check on him before I leave. Would you like to join me?"

"If you don't mind."

Greg appeared to be agitated at their appearance in his room.

"What's he doing here?" he demanded as he looked at Nash.

Nash stepped back but Tammy's hand reached for his arm to keep him there.

"Now, Greg," Tammy soothed. "You know Nash Adams. We're both on your side. We want to help you. We care about you."

Greg thrashed for a few more moments.

"Lay still," Tammy warned. "You'll pull out your IV."

She placed her hand on his shoulder to calm him.

"Tammy," he reached for her arm to express his remorse. "You've always been good to me. Too good for me."

He started to cry again as the medication began to take effect and Tammy patted his hand until she took it and gently tucked it back under the sheet.

"I'm sorry, Tammy. So sorry."

With that confession, Greg Carter closed his eyes.

"I believe he'll sleep now," Tammy told Nash.

As Tammy and Nash tiptoed from the room, he whispered to her.

"What was he apologizing for?" he asked.

"I don't know," she answered. "Who knows? He probably didn't even know what he was saying."

After reporting to Louie about Greg Carter's apparent nervous breakdown, Nash set out in search of Margaret Shore Hastings. He located her at the Woods residence on Hickory Lane.

"No, I don't recall telling anyone other than Tammy and the three children that Lindy was coming home. And I certainly had no idea she had taken an earlier flight."

"Is there anyway anyone could have overheard your conversations with the children or Tammy?" Nash needed to know.

"I talked to the three children on the phone," she said, "from my apartment. I dropped in on Tammy and told her at her apartment. I can't imagine anyone overhearing our conversation."

Content that Margaret was telling the truth, Nash headed back to his office where he lost himself in paperwork until Anne Meijer knocked on the door.

"What is it, Anne? You look upset," he said as he folded up the papers he had been working on.

"I am," she whispered and looked over her shoulder at the dark hallway.

"What's going on? Come, sit down and talk to me."

Anne took the chair, but pulled it closer to Nash's desk and continued to whisper.

"You know how I've been suspicious of the two men who've rented the room next to yours?"

"Yeah, I remember you telling me about that," Nash agreed.

"Well, I've been watching and I've come to some conclusions," she said once again casting a long look at the hallway.

Nash got up from his chair and closed the door.

"What conclusions?" he asked.

"I think they are only in that room when you are here in your office," she breathed a huge sigh to have divulged that information.

"Are they there now?" Nash questioned.

"No, not now," she explained. "I made sure of that before I came up here."

"Well, there you have it. What you've observed just may be a coincidence..." Nash started to say but Anne immediately began shaking her head.

"There's more?" Nash was patient.

"I did something terrible," Anne was on the verge of tears.

Nash put his hand on her shoulder to comfort her.

"I doubt that you could possibly do anything terrible," he consoled.

She nodded her head.

"I did. Papa would be furious with me if he knew," she confessed.

"How about you just tell me what happened and let me be the judge of that."

Choking back the tears, she motioned for him to come closer.

"I watched them leave," she began.

"The men?" he clarified.

"Yes. And then...and then...and then I took Papa's keys and I crept up the stairs and I opened the door to that room."

Nash realized for Anne to do something like that would be a traumatic experience for her.

"But I had to find out for myself," she whispered.

"What did you find out, Anne?"

"I saw equipment," she told him. "I don't know exactly what it is, but lots of equipment...wires and a tape recorder and some other things."

Nash tried to absorb what she was telling him.

"Anne," he said, "by chance would you still have the keys?"

She dug in her skirt pocket.

"I kept them because I thought you might want to see for yourself...but if Papa ever finds out..."

"We'll be quiet," Nash said as he pulled a flashlight out of his desk drawer; and taking the keys, he motioned her to follow him.

Quietly opening the door to his office and carefully checking to make sure there was no sign of activity from downstairs, they made their way to the door of the room next to his.

"Hold the flashlight," he whispered to Anne who steadied a beam of light on the door lock.

Sounds of the key turning in the lock seemed to penetrate the air. Nash turned the doorknob and reached for the flashlight. Stepping into the coolness of the now unlocked room, he felt Anne's hand on his shoulder.

"You don't have to come with me," he told her.

"I want to," she whispered.

Nash scanned the room with the glow from the flashlight. Anne was indeed correct in her assessment. Some things were becoming clear to Nash as he examined the electronics.

Nash turned to Anne.

"Anne, would you go back to my office, close the door and just start talking in a normal voice?"

"What do you want me to say?" she asked.

"It doesn't matter. Just keep talking for a long time."

He turned the flashlight so she could make her way to the door and out into the hallway. Then he sat to work. Before long, he had figured out what he needed to know. Putting everything back the way he'd found it, he tiptoed out the room, locked the door and returned to his office where Anne was reciting a passage from the Constitution of the United States. She stopped when she saw him and her eyes opened wide.

Nash closed the door and Anne hurried to his side.

"You were right," Nash said. "Your suspicions were valid."

"But what?"

"It appears someone has been listening to conversations that have taken place in this office," he explained. "We need to find the transmitter...the bug."

He immediately began searching.

"What am I looking for?" Anne asked.

"Something small, round, metal."

It took some time, but they finally found it attached to one of the picture frames.

"What shall we do now?" Anne wanted to know.

"Nothing," Nash answered. "Nothing right now. We might just have some use for it. From now on, they will only hear what we want them to."

"Is it too late for me to make a house call?" Nash asked Tammy.

"Well, I guess not," Tammy stammered. "Is this important? Have you uncovered some new information?"

"We'll talk when I get there. I'm about ten minutes away."

"I'll be expecting you."

Tammy hung up the phone and wondered what in the world could be so important as to warrant a call at this time of the evening. This was a day that appeared to never stop for her. First Greg's breakdown and then dealing with the business and the hospital. The last thing Tammy Woods wanted to do was to entertain Nash Adams, or anyone else for that matter.

But when Tammy answered Nash's knock on the door, she immediately caught the intenseness in his manner.

"What in the world...?" she began.

Nash put his fingers to his mouth to silence her. He pulled out his notebook and pen and started writing.

I think there may be a bug in this apartment and everything we say may be monitored.

Tammy's eyes grew big as she mouthed, "What should we do?"

"Keep up regular conversation," Nash whispered and started looking.

He found it neatly tucked under the coffee table as he and Tammy exchanged pleasantries. Beckoning to Tammy to come into the hallway where they could talk freely, he left the bug where he found it.

"You'll have to decide what you want to do about it," he told her.

"How did you know?" she asked.

"My office was bugged," he admitted. "Someone knew about Lindy coming into town. Your mother said she called the children by phone and had talked personally with you. When I found one in my office, I thought perhaps your apartment had been bugged as well. Now, we need to determine who might have been here to plant it."

"I'm not here a lot. My mother, Raoul. I had the living room painted right after I moved in so painters were here. There was a plumber a couple of weeks ago. Can't think of anyone else."

"Think about it and keep your eyes and ears open," Nash cautioned. "I think it is all tied together somehow."

"What was in the envelope?" Nash asked as he sat across from the blonde Lindy.

"Well, that was really strange. I forgot all about it until I got back from the restaurant that night. When I opened it, there was a note that just said, You are not alone. I don't know if it was meant to be consoling or threatening."

"Have you ever had any connections to Greg Carter?"

"As you know, he was my father's business partner so we saw them socially."

"Did your Dad and Mr. Carter pal around together? I mean outside of the office world?"

Lindy thought for a few minutes.

"Yes. They often played racketball and they went hunting up at the cabin in Colorado several times."

"Would you say Greg Carter was familiar with the hunting cabin?"

"Oh, yes. He and Zoe often vacationed in that part of Colorado. Yes, I'd say Greg Carter was very familiar with the cabin."

Chapter 22

It was taco day at the little walk-in restaurant located near the Woods & Carter offices and Nash was meeting Katie for lunch. The warm spring weather had turned into a pleasant June day and a number of people were taking advantage of that by being outside. Nash and Katie sat at one of the sidewalk tables, not unlike those in front of the Meijer deli.

"Office keeping busy with Mr. Carter gone?" Nash asked as he manipulated a taco in preparation for getting it into his mouth without losing its contents.

"Actually, I enjoy Mrs. Woods being there. She's a lot calmer about things. Plus she seems to have a good head on her shoulders, knows how to make decisions. But I heard this morning that Mr. Carter has been released from the hospital and should be back to work on a limited basis. We'll see how that goes."

"Yeah," Nash nodded.

Katie stopped long enough to take a bite of taco and a sip of her soft drink before she continued.

"An interesting item came across my desk this morning," she said, wiping taco from her mouth with the paper napkin.

"What's that?"

"Well, a lot of bills pass through my hands...things that have been purchased for the business, for the office. And I usually know exactly what they are for as people give me memos about things that may be coming due. But this was a strange one. It was for some electronic equipment. You know, tape recorder, microphones, receivers, speaker... things like that. I called the company and they informed me that Greg Carter had signed for those things. Just kinda weird that he didn't tell me. But then I guess he's had a lot on his mind recently."

Katie continued to devour the tacos. Nash stopped eating and looked at Katie. He appeared to be calm, but his heart began to race.

Was this the information that would finally link Greg Carter to the murder of Stephen Woods?

Katie looked up from her meal.

"You okay?" she asked.

"Oh, yeah, sure. Yes, that is kinda strange," he agreed.

Raoul stood at the door to Tammy Woods' apartment, several bags of food in his hands. Tammy had agreed to see him for a short time this evening; and since Tammy was tired and didn't want to leave to go to a restaurant, he had suggested eating in instead. She'd had little time for him lately and he resented that. Things were not working quite like he had imagined. He had envisioned spending intimate time with her, but she always seemed to keep him at arm's length; and that only made him want her more. Raoul was a man used to having or buying anything he desired. Tammy was the one thing he couldn't have and that drove him crazy and caused him to fly off the handle, to make poor decisions and say and do things he regretted later. But tonight would be different. He would show her how kind and understanding he could be this evening.

He'd been patient. He'd given her space. Well, perhaps tonight would be a turning point in their relationship. Balancing the packages and a bouquet of flowers he had picked up at a spur of the moment, he freed a hand to press the doorbell.

"Come in," Tammy said as she opened the door.

She was dressed in an evening robe and slippers. She allowed him to kiss her cheek as she took packages from his arms.

"Thanks for coming by. I really did not wish to go out tonight."

"Anything for you, my pet," he purred.

"Let's just eat here on the sofa," she said as she placed the food on the coffee table very near the bug planted on the bottom of the table.

She carried on conversation with him, being cautious of anything that might be recorded, asking him about his time on the yacht and pretending to be interested in his latest business trip. She shared with him about her day with Greg at the office and the hospital. She was perhaps hungrier than she thought. The food tasted especially good. Well, maybe she hadn't eaten much that day, or maybe not at all.

Finally it came down to dessert, the cute little pastries she loved so much. Touching that he remembered.

"So how long will Greg Carter be in the hospital?" he asked.

"The doctor said probably a day or two."

"They should keep him longer. I don't trust him and I don't like you working with him."

It was the first time all evening he had felt threatened and anger began to rise within him. Tammy sensed the emotion and attempted to change the subject.

"You know, Raoul..." she began and then let the sentence drift.

"What is it, Tammy?"

"Well, I know you'll think I'm crazy, but sometimes I feel like I'm not alone."

"Well, you'll never be alone as long as I'm around. You know I want to take care of you, Tammy. You know how I feel."

"Oh, I know that. That's not what I mean. I mean like maybe I'm being spied on."

"You think someone is following you? I've got men. If you want, I can..."

Tammy pretended to dismiss the idea.

"No, not following me. Guess I'm just being silly. Maybe just being paranoid."

"No, no. Go on. You can tell me anything. I think you're an intelligent person and take anything you tell me seriously."

"Oh, I know, Raoul. You are always there for me."

It was at that moment she realized how much she did not want Raoul to be anywhere for her, unless it was a long way away. But she continued.

"I just feel like someone is listening to my thoughts. Never mind. As I said, I'm just being silly. Raoul, could you be a dear? I am really tired tonight."

Raoul stood. He would do anything for this woman...anything for this woman.

"Of course. You've been under a lot of stress. I understand," Raoul said as he headed for the door, proud to have kept his emotions under control. "Can I do anything else for you?"

"No, thank you. I'll be asleep before you get to your car," she smiled.

"Goodnight then," Raoul said as he reached for her and hugged her and did not feel the resistance she felt.

"Oh, and Raoul," Tammy added. "Thank you so much for coming to Lindy's rescue. Strange you came along just at that time."

She watched his face for any reaction and saw none.

"Yes," he explained. "A really good thing I came along when I did."

She agreed.

"Oh, yes, what a coincidence," she smiled.

Tammy closed the door behind him, stopping to pick up a piece of paper Raoul had dropped from his jacket pocket.

"Oh, Raoul, you dropped something," she called out but he was gone.

Opening the paper, she read: Casey's Automotive Specialties.

The delicatessen was closed. Nash and Anne sat at one of the tables, having seen the two men in suits climb the stairs to "their office".

"We'll fool them a bit and stay down here," he whispered to his young energetic self-appointed assistant. "They won't overhear anything tonight."

Anne smiled shyly but nervously at the man she admired.

"Here's some paper and a pencil," Nash said. "Let's make a list."

They discussed in low tones the facts until they had built a case. Greg Carter was the most likely suspect. College. Jealous of Stephen's academic success. Then losing Tammy to Stephen. He knew the hunting cabin in Colorado and was familiar with guns and hunting. On the exact days Stephen was killed, Greg had been missing from the office, supposedly ill. He was having an affair with Stephen's wife, Gina; and getting rid of Stephen would mean getting rid of an obstacle in his relationship with her. And then there had been the argument between Greg and Stephen in the office just a few days before the murder. Plus his behavior had been that of a man hiding a terrible secret.

"I think Greg Carter is our man," Nash whispered.

"It certainly looks that way," Anne agreed.

She put her hand on Nash's arm.

167

"Shh," she said. "Someone's coming."

Flipping off the light switch as she passed by, she pulled Nash behind the meat counter and they crouched together in the darkness as they watched the two men in suits descend the stairs and go out the front door of the delicatessen.

Nash moved quickly.

"Where are you going?" Anne whispered.

"I'm going to follow them," Nash replied.

"I'm going with you," Anne said as she moved behind him across the dimly lit deli floor and into the night air.

Just as they reached Nash's car, they saw the black SUV pull around the corner. There was no time to lose. At first, when Nash turned the corner, he thought perhaps the SUV had made a successful get away, but then he spied it up ahead and he proceeded to weave in and out of traffic until he had them safely in his sight. Anne sat quietly in the passenger seat, the knuckles on her right hand turning white as she grasped the door handle.

Nash was becoming all too familiar with this part of town. It appeared the SUV was headed for one of two places...either The Gateway Hotel or the pier. At that time, two cars ahead of him stopped and the car in front of him did not and Nash was caught behind a fender bender. He strained to see where the SUV went and searched for a way around the accident. Apparently they were hemmed in so they sat quietly as night descended on the scene of the accident.

Nash sighed and looked at his young companion. She really did look out of place in her print dress and old-fashioned shoes; but, regardless of her outward appearance, Nash was beginning to appreciate the beauty that existed within her.

"Looks like we lost 'em," he said. "You okay?"

Anne's face was a chalky white as she stared straight ahead.

"Yes," she finally answered. "Yes, I am alright. And what you told me about being a private investigator? It's true. Most of the time it's boring, but sometimes it's very exciting."

Nash laughed at her remarkable innocence.

"How about I treat you to an ice cream sundae? And then I'd better get you back to the deli. That is, whenever we get out of this mess."

Car horns were honking at a terrific rate of speed as angry drivers, intent on reaching their destinations, expressed their annoyance at being delayed.

Chapter 23

When Anne wasn't spending her summer working in the delicatessen, she was helping Nash in the upstairs office. Clients were beginning to increase and Anne had appointed herself as Nash's unofficial secretary. An old table she found in the basement became her desk. So it was only natural that Anne answered the telephone when it rang.

"Good morning," she said as she picked up the receiver. "You have reached the office of Nash Adams, personal investigator."

Nash looked up from his paper work and smiled. Anne was certainly the efficient young lady.

"Yes, yes he is. May I say who is calling, please? Edna? Yes, thank you."

She handed the phone to Nash.

"Nash Adams here," he said.

"Mr. Adams. This is Edna...you remember...the waitress from the diner in Colorado?"

"Oh, yes, I remember."

"Well, it come to me yesterday when we were talkin' about it here at the diner. There was a second fella that was in here about the same time as the one that got killed. I just remembered and then I looked and found your card 'cause you said if I ever thought of anything more, I should give you a call."

"Wonderful. Do you think you would be able to identify him from a photograph?" Nash asked as his pulse ran rampant at the thought of finally putting this case to rest.

"Oh, yes, I remember him real good," was the reply. "He asked some questions that were kinda strange. And this is a small town. Anyone new is memorable. I think he might be linked to the murder."

"Can I send you a photo?"

There was a pause on the other end of the line. Of course not. Edna in a small town in Colorado would not be savvy to technology.

"I'll catch the first flight out there," Nash told her.

"I'll be here," Edna replied.

"Thanks. Thank you, Edna," Nash said hurriedly as he hung up the phone.

He immediately went to the picture that hung on the wall and retrieved the bug planted there, walked to the aquarium Margaret Hastings had insisted upon and dropped it in the tank of startled fish.

Meanwhile, in the room next door, Stokes sat listening to the new turn of events.

"Get the boss on the phone," he told his companion. "I got news he's gonna want to hear."

The smile disappeared from his face when he heard nothing but a blurred gurgling sound coming from the earpiece. He jerked it from his ear.

"What the..." he said, violently shaking the earpiece.

Meanwhile, Nash was busy with details.

"I think we've got him," he told Anne. "Edna, the waitress at the diner remembers a second man being in town about the same time as Stephen Woods was there and I'm willing to bet she will be able to identify Greg Carter. I'm going to need..."

But Anne was ahead of him, already taking down photos and placing them in a manila envelope.

Nash listened as the phone on Louie's desk rang seven times.

"Come on, answer," he said anxiously.

"Louie here," came the voice he needed to hear.

"It's me...Nash. I just got a call from the waitress in Colorado. She says there was a second man in town about the same time as Stephen Woods...asking questions...and she can identify him. I'm going out there. I think you will be getting a call from me real soon to pick up Greg Carter."

"Okay, man, I'll be on the alert. He shouldn't be too hard to locate. I'll get right on it."

A second call was to the airport. He could catch a flight at 1:15. He would have to hurry.

"Mom, grab my overnight and throw in a change of clothes just in case I have to stay over. I'm headed to Colorado. I'll explain later."

His adrenalin had kicked in as he called Katie.

"Katie here," came her voice with the lilt in it.

"Katie, this is Nash," he began.

"Oh, surprise. Good to hear your voice."

"Yeah," he hurried on with his message. "I've got a hot tip in Colorado. I'm flying out there in an hour or so. Is Greg Carter in the office?"

"Yes. I don't think he'll be here long though. This is his first day back and I understand the doctor doesn't want him to put in many hours for a while."

"Katie, don't let him leave. Do whatever you have to do, but keep Greg Carter in the office."

"But..." she protested.

"I'll explain later."

He hung up the phone and took the manila envelope from Anne's hands.

"Thanks," he said as he headed for the door.

"Don't worry," Anne smiled. "I'll take care of things here while you're gone."

Nash stopped at the door, thinking once again of the men next door.

"Be careful, Annie," he warned. "Don't take any chances."

He closed the door to his office behind him and took the stairs at a run on his way to pick up his overnight and head to the airport.

"Boss, the kid thinks he has the murderer and he's headed to Colorado. But my equipment went silent so I don't know anything else."

Stokes listened carefully to the voice on the other end of the phone.

"No, I don't know the number of the flight. I told you things went dead here. But today, I think."

"Yeah, he's gone, but the girl from downstairs is still in his office."

Stokes was listening to instructions.

"Yeah, we can do that. What do you want us to do with her?"

"Okay, got it!"

Stokes turned to his accomplice.

"Come on, we got a job to do," he said as he headed for the door.

In the room next door, Anne picked up the ringing phone.

"Oh, hi, Katie," she said. "No, he's already gone. No problem."

The call hadn't been disconnected when the door to Nash's office opened and two men came through it.

"What do you want?" she said, her voice reflecting the fear she felt.

"Anne," Katie said into the still-connected phone call. "Anne, what's wrong? What's happening?"

But there was no answer.

Katie's next phone call was to Louie down at the precinct. She shared the information with him and her concern that something may have happened to Anne Meijer. He agreed to check it out.

Terror struck in Anne's chest as the men approached her. She attempted to protest as the desk chair overturned on the floor. Although she reached for one man's arm and dug her fingernails into his skin, she was quickly overpowered, gagged and pushed and half carried down the steps. The deli was abuzz with lunchtime traffic and too busy to perhaps notice any out of the ordinary activity. Stokes' partner checked; and feeling they would be undetected, they hurried Anne out the back way and into the black SUV.

Although tears threatened to escape her eyes and her heart pounded in her chest, Anne tried to remember everything Nash had been teaching her along the way. What was it he had said? If you should ever find yourself in a hostage situation, use your senses to keep track of where you are. Once in the back of the car, they blindfolded her, but not before she noted which way the car was headed. It was facing north. As the vehicle made progress, she tried desperately to keep track of the moves. Started north. Turned right so must be going east. North again. Then east again. Then a series of bumps and she lost track of where they were. Slowed. Came to a complete stop. A breeze hit her face as they helped her out of the car and then she heard the sound of water lapping at the pier. Then the unsteadiness of the boat under her feet as they boarded. She was on a boat and quite possibly at the marina. She was sure of that, but what good would that do if she couldn't share her information with rescuers?

She heard muffled voices, something about doing a good job and had they found out anything else? She couldn't make out their answer or identify the third voice.

She did the only thing she knew how to do. She began making as much noise as she could with the gag still in her mouth.

"Go ahead and take the blindfold off," came the instructions. "But wait until I'm gone. I don't want her to be able to identify me."

She didn't recognize the voice. There was a pause and then she felt the blindfold release. She continued making noise.

"Should we find out what she's trying to say?" one of the men asked.

"I don't know. What if she yells?"

One man approached her.

"If I remove the gag, you have to promise me you won't yell. If you do, you'll wish you hadn't," he threatened.

Noticing the size of his fists, Anne had no alternative but to believe he would make good on his threats so she nodded in agreement.

Once the gag was removed from her mouth, Anne felt her lungs expand. Perspiration coated her face and her throat was parched.

"Could I please have a glass of water?" she asked as she fought the dryness in her throat.

That seemed an easy enough request and it was granted.

"Thank you," she said meekly.

At first she sat quietly, afraid to look any further than straight ahead of her. She knew she was sitting on a cushioned seat near the edge of the boat while her captures sat at a small table directly in front of her. She made no move to get up and eventually the two men picked up a deck of cards from the table and became engrossed in a game.

She chose to concentrate on the two men in front of her. She needed to be clear if she was called on to identify them. One was fat with a receding hair line and beady eyes and seemed to be the follower. And there was a tattoo of some kind on his right forearm. The one who was probably in charge was a short man with dark hair and a mustache and a goatee. He wore a large ring on his right hand and had a habit of cracking his knuckles. And he had red scratch marks on his forearm.

Her hands were trembling and the muscles in her stomach were doing sit-ups all by themselves. Telling herself she needed to breathe and try to relax, she concentrated on the things she could see. Clues could be in the details. Be aware of your surroundings at all times, Nash had told her. If only she had followed that advice a short time ago, she might not be in this predicament now.

Again Anne tried to concentrate on her surroundings. What she surmised was that this was not a normal boat. This was a fancy one, a yacht. Today's newspaper lay on the cushion next to her. A well-stocked bar was behind the men at the table. There was no movement of a boat under power, just the quiet rocking of a boat moored at the dock. It did not appear the vessel was being prepared to sail. That was good. Her pulse quickened at the thought of being adrift. How would Nash find her then? There was a porthole fairly close to her, but she couldn't see much out of it and the one on the opposite side only revealed a blue sky overhead. Well, at this point, she couldn't think of a way out, so she would just sit quietly and wait for an opportunity. Nash would surely find her...but not until he returned from Colorado. Did he even know she was missing? Once again terror overtook her. She fought the tears that formed again in her eyes and felt the sinking feeling envelop her stomach...again. Hurry, Nash, hurry!

Louie did not want to alarm the Meijer family. Although they saw him come in and hurry up the stairs, they probably would assume he was just visiting a bit with Nash. Louie found the door to Nash's office unlocked and some papers strewn on the floor. Nash had told him about his office being bugged. Louie searched for it. He finally spied it in the fish tank. But if it was bugged, surely those listening were close by. Louie entered the hallway. No other rooms up here other than the two offices and a rest room at the end of the hallway. He tried the door next to Nash's. Locked. Taking his kit from his pocket, he tripped the lock and turned on the light. As he looked around, he knew Nash was right. Any conversations in Nash's office were being monitored. He sorted through the assortment of fast food cartons and paper cups until he found a cell phone which had been accidently left behind in their haste to leave. Surely he could retrieve some information from that. Tucking it in his pocket, he closed and locked the door and made his way back to the precinct.

Nash's plane landed on schedule and he wasted no time in getting to the diner where Edna was indeed waiting on him. He extended his hand to the middle-aged woman with the dyed hair.

"I really appreciate your call, Edna. I think you may be able to clear up this entire matter for us," he said.

"Glad to do it," she replied. "I don't know why I didn't think of it a few weeks ago when you were here."

She gestured to one of the booths covered in a 1950's red plastic upholstery. He followed her there and sat across from her.

"The important thing is that you did remember," Nash encouraged. "I brought photographs with me; and if you can identify the man, it will certainly help our case."

A customer walked by.

"You workin' today, Edna?" he asked.

"Takin' my break," she replied.

Then by way of explanation to Nash, she said, "I have certain customers that prefer my service."

She smiled.

"I been watin' tables here for quite a few years and I got my regulars."

It was Nash's turn to smile.

"And we don't get too many strangers around these parts. That's why they stand out in my mind."

Nash proceeded to dump the photos from the manila envelope where Anne had put them. He hadn't realized she had sent most of the ones that were on his wall back in the office. He sorted through them and made sure the photo of Greg Carter was visible.

Edna sorted through them and picked up one to closely examine it.

"This one," she exclaimed.

Nash was shocked

"Not this man?" he asked.

"Oh, no, that's not the one," Edna denied. "I'm sure. It was this man."

He was sure Edna would identify Greg Carter and he would be on his way back in time to see Greg brought in for questioning. He slumped back in his seat.

Edna began to sort through the remaining photos, commenting on the beauty of the ladies in them, but came back to the same picture.

"This is the man. This is him right here!" she reiterated.

Nash took the photo from her hand. It was a photo of Raoul.

"You'd swear to it?" he asked her.

"Oh, yes. I am positive," she said in a firm manner.

Nash needed to hurry.

"Excuse me," he said. "I need to make a phone call."

He rushed outside where the cool air of the Colorado mountains smacked him in the face. It was in stark contrast to the flush of excitement he felt. Relief was the emotion he felt when he heard Louie's voice.

"It's me," Nash gasped.

"Yeah. You got positive identification? I'm ready to pick up Carter," Louie said.

Nash knew the words he wanted to form in his own mouth, but his heightened senses sprang ahead of him. He gasped for breath.

"Not Carter. Carter's the wrong one!" he blurted out. Nash was breathless. "It's Raoul!"

There was a silence.

"I'm on it," Louie assured him.

"Good."

"Nash..." Louie was debating on whether or not he should tell Nash about Anne's abduction.

"Nash...they've got Anne," he said simply.

A sinking feeling came over Nash and his knees began to buckle.

"You okay, man?" Louie continued.

"Yeah. Yeah, I'm okay," came the unsteady answer.

"How? Why?" he demanded.

"Must have taken her right after you left."

A wave of nausea passed over his body.

"Don't worry. We'll find her," Louie promised.

Don't worry? If anything happened to Anne...it would be Nash's fault. She was his responsibility.

"Find Raoul. He's the key," Nash answered.

Chapter 24

Nash was in his car, speeding from the airport towards town.

"I've talked with Tammy Woods," Louie was telling him on his cell phone. "She doesn't know for sure where he is, but she told us a couple of places to look. I'm on my way to the marina right now."

Nash hung up his phone and made a U turn while cars honked and drivers shook their fists at him. Nash needed to get to Anne. If anything happened to that girl...

By the time he reached the parking lot at the marina, there were already police cars there blinking red and blue lights and Nash saw several officers in uniform positioned near their squad cars. Spotting Louie, he ran up to him.

"What do we know?" he asked anxiously.

"We just got here. No sign of activity on the yacht as far as we can see. Might be deserted. Do you think Tammy would alert him?"

"From everything I've seen, I doubt it."

"Good. Hughes, get me the bull horn."

In seconds, the request was granted and Louie prepared his speech.

"Raoul Hoffer, we know you are in there. Come out peacefully. We just want to talk with you."

Nash scanned the decks of the yacht, searching for any sign of movement. He saw none. Were they too late? Had the yacht been vacated? Where would they take her and would they hurt her? No, surely Raoul was smarter than that.

Inside the yacht, Anne had heard Louie's voice coming through the air but what was an instant of hope was daunted by her hands and mouth being confined again. It was uncomfortable at best and she struggled as she was lifted to her feet only to be pushed into a dark enclosure. She was laying on her side and it was impossible to move her body as the position caused her muscles to tense.

There was no response to Louie's demand. A Cadillac pulled into the parking lot and two men in suits got out of it. Nash recognized them as being well-known attorneys in the area, attorneys who had been linked to organized crime. When Raoul saw them approach, he came out of the cabin of the yacht.

"What can I do for you fellas?" he asked calmly.

"We'd just like for you to come down to the precinct and answer a few questions," Louie explained.

"What's this about?" one of the lawyers asked as he approached the scene.

Without looking at him, Raoul continued.

"Sure. Sure thing. I haven't done anything. My friends here (meaning the lawyers) would be glad to accompany me. Just so we keep things even, you know," Raoul smiled.

Raoul was cool. After all, in his line of business, it was not unusual for him to be hand in hand with the police force, not necessarily in a friendly manner, however.

When Raoul was close enough, Louie had more questions.

"Who else is aboard the yacht?" he wanted to know.

"Just a couple of my men," was the answer.

"We might need to see them as well," Louie said. "Tell them to come on out."

"Sure," Raoul was calm. "I always like to cooperate with the police. I'm a law abiding citizen, you know."

Raoul's cool manner caused anger to well up in Nash's already emotional body. He just wanted to grab Raoul and start punching.

A calm and smooth Raoul turned to the yacht and called out.

"Come on, fellas," he said. "The good detective wants to talk to you as well."

Two men dressed in black emerged from the yacht. By this time, a crowd was beginning to gather.

"Anybody else inside?" Louie asked.

"No. See for yourself."

Nash was beginning to panic. No sign of Anne and they were willing to let the policemen search the yacht? Did that mean they were holding Anne somewhere else? Or worse? He followed the police officers onto the yacht, his stomach sick with fear, while Louie dealt with the lawyers over taking Raoul into custody. They had walked the decks and the cabin of the yacht twice now and still there was no sign of Anne. The officers were ready to begin a search of the water when Nash heard a faint sound coming from the edge of the craft.

"I hear something. Do you hear that?" he shouted and they all stopped to listen.

"I don't hear anything," one officer said. "Nash, you're too close to this situation. Perhaps you'd best stay on dry land."

Nash was filled with disappointment. But as the officers turned to leave, Nash heard the sound again. This time one of the officers heard it as well.

"Coming from here," the young officer said. "Help me."

Together they began tearing cushions from their resting places.

"We need something to pry with," one of them suggested.

Some piece of the ship sufficed and they began prying at the seats. Finally, the lid was lifted and crouched underneath was a very scared and relieved Anne Meijer.

"Be careful with her," Nash cautioned.

The officers lifted her out. Her hands and feet were tied and her mouth was taped. Nash gently removed the tape while the officers freed her hands and feet. She collapsed in his outstretched arms and he held her against his chest as she sobbed and he struggled with tears of his own.

"It's okay. It's okay," Nash soothed as her sobs subsided. "You're safe now. I'm so sorry, Annie."

He led the still trembling Anne from the yacht, not ignoring the look of relief on his friend, Louie's face.

They watched as Raoul and his two henchmen were taken away followed closely by his attorneys who were already strategizing about the terms of his release.

Nash helped Anne into his car. He listened patiently as she relayed her story, about how the two men had burst into the office and abducted her, how she listened carefully for any clues that would help in her escape. Yes, she could identify both men, but she had never seen Raoul. She'd only heard his voice. They talked for a long time before Nash was convinced she was settling down a bit.

"You know you'll have to go down to the precinct to answer a lot of questions for the police, don't you?" he began.

She shook her head.

"I know," her voice trembled. "But I want to. I want to help put this man behind bars."

Nash reached for her hand,

"I am so sorry, Annie," he said. "I should never have left you in the office alone. I should have insisted you go back downstairs to your family before I ever left."

"I'm okay," she told him. "But the next time you try to tell me that being a personal investigator is boring, I'll have something to say about it."

"Guess you're going to put some of this in your summer assignment for your teacher, too, eh?" he teased.

"Oh, for sure. I doubt that anyone else will have such an entertaining paper."

They both were able to laugh about that. And then it was time to take Anne back to her home.

Chapter 25

They were all gathered in the living room of the spacious house on Hickory Lane...Cliff, Susan, Lindy, Candy, Tammy, Grandmother Hastings, Nash and Louie.

"I can't believe Raoul would do such a thing," Lindy said. "He was always good to me."

"Because he wanted you on his side, so to speak," Nash explained. "Giving you the use of the yacht, those kinds of things. Anything to make himself look good in your eyes. But always something he could use to his own advantage."

"But he rescued me the day I came back to town," Lindy defended.

"Yes, and did you find it the least bit strange that he came along just as you were let go?" Louie chimed in.

"Are you saying he planned it that way?" Lindy continued her innocence and shock at the information being put forth.

"It looks like it."

"But how do you explain the taxi cab?" she wanted to know.

"We thought the vehicle belonged to Greg Carter which would implicate him. Well, actually it did belong to Zoe Carter, but it had been sold. We were sure that linked Carter to the crime. But we found out that Zoe's car had been purchased...not under Raoul's real name, of course...but he was behind it."

Nash took over further explanation.

"Your mother found a receipt that dropped out of Raoul's pocket from a car specialty store. That's where he had the cab window installed. And Raoul had signed for it so that is proof of his involvement."

"He really was manipulating everyone," Cliff added.

"That was his hook," Louie explained. "It was all about control and hatred and jealousy. He wanted to be close to all of you children as a way of getting to your mother. And he tried to find something in each one of you that he could use."

"It doesn't surprise me at all," Margaret Shore Hastings said. "I never did like the man."

"Well, we certainly know how you feel, Grandmother," Cliff added. "So what do you mean when you say he wanted something on each one of us he could use?"

"With you, Cliff," Louie continued, "it was the gambling. Who do you think financed you to get back in the game? He had you right in his pocket, an IOU he could call in if necessary."

"That was his plan...to put everyone he knew in a position where they were beholding to him or where he could control them by some means or other."

"I was so blind," Cliff admitted.

"And I can't believe you went back after I bailed you out," Grandmother Hastings scolded.

"I'm sorry, grandmother," Cliff apologized.

Margaret Shore Hastings rolled her eyes.

"Remember this experience, Cliff, because if I ever..."

With that Grandmother Hastings' voice elevated with an unspoken threat.

"Don't tell me you thought you were actually good at gambling, Cliff," Susan spit the words at her brother.

"I did. I was really convinced I could win."

"I didn't know any of this," Tammy said quietly. "How could I have been so out of touch?"

"What did he have on you, Susan?" Cliff was quick to ask, perhaps to take himself out of the limelight.

"Actually, Susan was the last one he was working on," Louie informed. "There were several luncheons between the two, but we think he hadn't found what he was looking for yet."

A smug look came over Susan's face.

"That's everyone but Candy," she said. "What did our little sister do?"

Candy had become extremely nervous during the conversation. Frequent glances filled with panic and constant playing with her hair gave her away.

Nash was not without compassion.

"If Candy wants you to know, she can tell you. It's up to her," he said quietly.

"All eyes focused on the youngest sibling."

"Well," Grandma Hastings began, having a premonition about where this was going, "I don't think we need to worry about that right now. I'm just grateful that dreadful man is behind bars where he should have been a long time ago."

It was a valiant effort to turn the conversation, but a fruitless one.

"It's okay, grandmother," Candy said. "I think I know what Raoul knew about me."

Nash nodded his head in agreement and encouragement.

"All of you remember that some time ago I vacationed with Grandmother Hastings in Europe."

"Candy, you don't have to," Grandmother Hastings was compassionate with her youngest granddaughter.

"It's time," Candy continued, twisting a handkerchief in her hands as she did. "Well, I spent the time in Europe because I was pregnant."

She let that piece of news sink in as she watched each of her sibling's faces and their reaction to the truth. Lastly, she met her mother's eyes; and it was at that point the tears began to fall. Grandmother Hastings went to her side and put her arms around her.

"I stayed there 'til the baby was born... a little girl. I named her Stephanie...after Dad. She's been staying with some of Grandmother's friends. But I get to see her when I go for a visit. That's why I've visited grandmother so often this past year."

With that piece of news, Candy broke down and sobbed while others remained stunned.

Tammy went to her daughter and embraced her.

"Why didn't you tell us? We would have understood," she said.

"Would you?" Candy retorted. "How many of you would have really understood?" she sobbed.

It was best to remain silent.

Nash cleared his throat.

"Raoul often visited the little town and somehow found out about the baby. He also sent Candy frequent notes, anonymously of course, threatening to expose her secret. Just another way of controlling her if need be."

"But why?" Susan asked.

"We believe it all was an effort to get to your mother. Jealousy. She was the one thing he couldn't have, couldn't buy. He believed she was still in love with Stephen; and if he got rid of Stephen, she would turn to him. That didn't work out for him as you can see."

Tammy Woods stood.

"I apologize to all of you," she said. "Raoul was kind to me after the divorce, but I was not romantically interested in him. He had a terrible temper and I have been considering getting him out of my life. Obviously not soon enough. Yes, I did love your father. Always have; always will. But I am so sorry for bringing Raoul into your lives. Please forgive me."

Lindy was the first to move to the arms of her mother and was quickly joined by the other children while Margaret Shore Hastings sat back and nodded her head in approval.

"One last thing," Nash spoke up. "Lindy, you met a man at the marina restaurant and money exchanged hands. I never did figure out how that was connected to this case."

The blonde haired Lindy smiled.

"That's because it didn't have anything to do with it," she said. "I have a dear friend in France who is kind enough to let me stay at her villa when I'm there. She wouldn't take any money so I bought her a car as payment and had someone else do the business part of it for me. Simple explanation. However, I will admit it was someone Raoul put me in touch with. Now I shudder at the thought."

Nash nodded in agreement.

"Raoul's lawyers are slick and have gotten him out of one scrape after another, but I think we have him this time. I'll wager others may come forward when this gets out. We suspect his import/export business is a shield for other things. Raoul is a clever man and let others do his dirty work for him, but it was his gun that shot Stephen and ballistics will match the bullet to his gun. And we can place him in Colorado at the time of the shooting. We have his voice on the cell phone left behind next to my office and we have Anne's testimony. At the very least, we have him on the kidnapping. Anne can identify the voice and link the two men to him and that's a huge help."

"Well," Louie said, "I believe that pretty much wraps things up here. Hopefully Raoul will be put away for a long time. We certainly have him on kidnapping and murder charges and I suspect that more will surface as we go along."

Tammy turned her deep gray eyes, now red from crying, towards Nash.

186

"Thank you, Nash," she said. "I...we all...are grateful to you. And you too," she added as she shook hands with both Louie and Nash.

The children thanked them as well. Then Margaret Shore Hastings rose from her seat.

Shaking Nash's hand, she promised, "Just let me know if you need my help with anything else. I'll be available for consultation."

She smiled as did Nash.

"I'll keep that in mind," he said.

Chapter 26

It was good to sit around Ma's table with the family. It was also good to know that justice had been served with the apprehension of Raoul Hoffer. Nash shared the entire story, concluding with Anne's abduction and rescue.

"I can't believe it," Ted said, putting down his utensils and bringing his hands down on the table. "All those beautiful women and you let them slip right through your fingers?"

"Guess you're big brother is kinda slow, eh?" Nash grinned.

"There are things more important than looks, little brother," Midge said, giving Ted a stern look.

Before Ted was able to give a response that Midge knew would be sure to come, she continued.

"Of course, it takes a bit of maturity to come to that realization. And seeing as how it takes the male of the species longer to reach maturity, I guess you wouldn't know anything about that."

"Ooh, she put you in your place," Nash laughed.

Ted took more interest in the food on his plate.

"I'm so glad that Anne Meijer was safe. She seems like such a nice girl," Ma offered.

"She is," Nash agreed. "Just like a little sister to me. Plus she's been a lot of help. I just didn't want her to get hurt. I felt responsible for putting her in danger. She says she wants to continue working for me this summer, just for the experience...and for the paper she's writing for a summer assignment. She's bright and willing and..." looking at Ted, Nash added..."and not bad looking."

"Maybe I should meet her then," Ted was back in the conversation with his usual exuberance.

"Yeah, maybe," Nash smiled. "And with the new clients I've gotten the past couple of weeks, I may just keep her on, that is if her folks don't mind. She's very efficient."

Supper lasted longer than usual that night at the Adams' house. Floating through the air were the tinkling sounds of ice against glass and the sounds of loving melodic voices sharing with each other at the end of the day, frequently interrupted by the sounds of laughter.

The End

Thanks for reading my book. If you enjoyed this please leave a review. It is how new readers discover my books. Thank you so much. ~ G.L. Gracie

Books by G.L. Gracie

Amelia

The Rose Trilogy:

Ivy and Wild Roses

Sweet Primrose

The White Rose

Willow

Refuge from the Storm

When Magnolias Bloom

Countin' Stars

Murder Among The Rich

https://www.facebook.com/G.L.Gracie

G.L. Gracie has been writing since she was thirteen years old, creating short stories, plays and poetry. Now she is developing novels. She is the mother of three and lives in southwestern lower Michigan. She likes to build her characters around the simple things of life, those things that form us and make us what we are.

53747249R10107

Made in the USA
Charleston, SC
17 March 2016